CHESTER PARSONS is NOT a GORILLA

MARTYN FORD

90 YEARS OF EXCELLENCE

FABER & FABER

First published in 2019
by Faber & Faber Limited
Bloomsbury House, 74–77 Great Russell Street
London, WC1B 3DA

Typeset in Garamond by M Rules
Printed and bound by CPI Group (UK) Ltd, Croydon, CR0 4YY

A CIP record for this book is available from the British Library

ISBN 978–0–571–33223–6

2 4 6 8 10 9 7 5 3 1

Dear Harry,

Chapter 1

Scary Things

'Who are you?' the man asked.

That's a fairly big question, I thought.

Who are *you*?

Like, are you your brain? Or are you a thing that lives *in* your brain? Are you that little person who talks in your thoughts – if so, who are they talking to? Or is your entire body you? But then, if you lost a finger, you'd still be you, right? If your head was in a jar, would *that* be you? Hmmm ...

I stared back at him in silence, squinting.

'What's your name?' he asked, noticing that I'd disappeared in thought.

'Oh, sorry. Chester Parsons,' I said.

The man ticked a box next to my name and told me to go and sit at the back with the others. Taking a deep breath, I strolled towards the empty chair at the end of the row. I was auditioning for a TV advert – the role I had been given was 'Potato 1'. Yeah, that's right. A potato. I was playing the part of a potato. I think we should repeat that, so we're completely clear: I was playing the part of *a potato*.

The audition was being held at a proper theatre in London too, the real deal. Even though all the characters would be different vegetables, they were taking it very seriously. A few of the others stepped out onstage and read their lines. Carrot went first – she was a girl around my age – and then Broccoli, who must have been about fifteen, and finally Beetroot, who seemed to be the only adult here.

Then it was my turn.

The stage lights were bright as I stepped out of the shadows, past the thick red curtain. Above me there were ropes and more lights and that sort of backstage theatre stuff, which is all messy and covered in bits of tape. Smells of dust and lofts. And wood. Makes you somehow itchy after a while. Anyway, I walked into the centre of the stage, stood on a small cross on the floor, cleared my throat and began to read my line.

'Stop, Mrs Carrot,' I said, throwing my voice like an absolute pro. 'Stop this madness, stop in the name of the—'

'No, no, NO!' the director yelled from his seat in the middle of the stalls.

I lowered the script and looked into the darkness.

'You're moving wrong,' he said. 'You're a potato. *Walk* like a potato. Go again.' He clapped twice.

Frowning, I stepped out of sight, exhaled, then walked on to the stage again – this time waddling slightly with straight legs and my arms at my sides. Really, he'd given me an impossible task. Potatoes, as I'm sure you're aware, can't walk. Never have. Almost certainly never will.

Then it happened. Bang. It arrived. The Fear. That's the problem with criticism – it throws me off balance. Suddenly my heart was pumping, my mouth was dry. I felt like I was at the top on a rollercoaster and I'd just spotted a gap in the track.

Why would anyone want to put themselves through this? Well, the answer for me is: ever since I can remember I have wanted to be an actor. If you think about it, it's the only real job a kid can do. It doesn't matter how old you are – in fact, being young is sometimes an advantage. When they need someone to play a child in a TV show or a film or, in this case, an advert for a sandwich shop, the best person is an actual child. I can't think of another job you can start doing at any age. You want to be a policeman? Well, bad luck, kid, no one's going to hire an eleven-year-old policeman. You want to be a doctor? You obviously need to go to university first. You want to be a dragon tamer? No such job, you idiot. Get out of my office. But you want to be an actor? Well, crack on. Go to an audition. I *dare* you.

It's also the *best* job because it's something I do anyway – it's like getting paid for sleeping or eating. I love pretending to be other people and when we were younger it was pretty much all me and my sister did. Dressed up and pretended we were pirates or robots or characters from one of our favourite TV shows. Never been a potato though.

The only downside to acting is that auditions are totally, utterly, completely scary. Like, imagine the scariest thing you've *ever* done and then times it by fifty. And times *that* by sixty. And then add ghosts.

Stage fright is actually common – even famous actors you've heard of get it. For me it can be pretty serious – I freeze up, go all rigid like those goats that faint when you shout at them. (That's a real thing. Google it.)

So, there I was, standing all potatoey (or apparently not, according to the director) under the spotlight, trembling. All the confidence I'd pretended I have was gone. My armpits were damp. My face was hot. My stomach was making weird noises. And, worst of all, my thoughts were wandering, which happens a lot sadly.

Stop being nervous, I said in my head. This *isn't* scary.

Bears. Now *bears* are scary. Dying too, that's pretty scary. Crazy to think isn't it – that everyone is going to die one day. What other scary things are there? Guns – they'll kill ya. Bombs – blow you to pieces, terrible things. Spiders are fairly awful. Bees, let's not forget them – delicious vomit, sure, but they'll mess you up with that sting. Not as bad as wasps though. They're sugary terrorists, buzzing about bins and apple cores like little stripy nightmares. Imagine a wasp the size of a dog.

Dog-wasp.

'Um, Chester?' the director said.

I refocused and realised I had been standing silently on the stage for quite a while, listing scary things in my head.

'Sorry,' I said, coughing. Get it together, Chester, you clown. I tried again. 'Stop, Mr Beetroot—'

'Wrong!'

'Uh, I mean Mr Carrot. Sorry. I'm just nervous. Can I do the line again? OK ... Stop, uh, stop, Mr ...'

'Remove yourself from my field of vision,' the director said, waving a slack hand.

I did not get the part ...

'How did it go?' Amy was waiting for me outside the theatre. She had given me a lift in her new car – which was an interesting experience as she only passed her test last week.

'Not good.'

'Nerves?'

'I think so.'

'You should go to that guy. The one Mum was talking about.'

'What? No. I don't need therapy. I just get stage fright sometimes, it's totally normal.'

We walked round the back of the building to the car park. It was sunny – I still felt hot from The Fear.

Amy slowed down and turned to me. 'You said that sometimes you get so nervous you feel like you're on fire and that the entire universe is trapped inside your stomach and your blood has been replaced with boiling jam.'

'So?'

'Well, Chester, that doesn't *sound* normal,' Amy said. 'If you get this worried about a rubbish advert for a sandwich shop then how— Hang on, who puts potatoes in sandwiches? And broccoli too?'

'Oh yeah, good point.'

'Anyway, hypnotherapy might help.' Amy unlocked her car door. We both climbed in. It was like an oven.

'My point is,' she said, 'if you get this nervous about an audition you don't care that much about, how are you going to handle something like *Sword of Steel and Stone*? A role you really, really want to get?'

'I've told you, I've already got the part,' I said, winding down the window. 'Pretty much.'

Believe it or not, playing a potato in a sandwich advert is not the best role a budding young actor can get. The *best* role a budding young actor can get is a main character in the *Sword of Steel and Stone* movie.

The truth is, I have had two auditions for the part and there is a third next week. There are only two of us left: me and this other guy who is so obviously bad at acting it's actually embarrassing. Like, it's mean to let him in front of the camera. So I've basically got the part.

In fact, I am so sure that I've already told everyone at school I'm going to be in the movie. And people are excited. Of course they are – everyone loves the TV show, the games are awesome, the books are super popular and now finally it's going to be a film too. It'll be great. Next week's audition is just to make it official.

I guess the producers at Screentwist have to pretend it's fair, even though they've probably already made up their minds.

That evening I found Mum sitting at the dining table, drinking white wine and looking at letters. They were bills. We get a lot of bills lately. She seemed worried until she realised I was standing in the doorway.

'Hey hey, there's my little potato,' she said.

I shook my head.

'Oh well, their loss.' She swept up all the pieces of paper, stood and put them on the counter. 'Where's your sister?'

'Who knows? She drove off somewhere – said she was getting something for a video. Wasn't really listening.'

'Did she mention—'

'*Yes*, she did,' I huffed. 'And I told her – I don't need it. People who kidnap seagulls and speak to clouds need therapy, you know, like *crazy* people.'

'Chester, that's not true. All kinds of people need a little bit of help from time to time – there's no shame in it. You are so talented. It'd be awful if nerves held you back.'

'You know what makes me nervous?' I said. 'People constantly talking about me being nervous.'

'The final audition is *next week*. Dr Vladovski can teach you some really simple—'

'*Fine*, I'll go and see your amazing mind man, although I doubt it'll do any good.'

Really, if I was honest, I was actually kind of hoping this Dr Vladovski *could* help – because feeling anxious does suck.

And so that's what I did. I went to *therapy*. Mum booked an appointment for the following day, and Amy dropped me off in her stupid little car, which was still scary. In fact, it was getting worse, because she was getting *confident*. We jolted to a stop, my seat belt catching me as my head flung forwards.

'Hurrhhhhgghh,' I gasped. The engine stuttered and stalled. 'Thanks. I'm feeling calmer already.'

'It's the pedal, this one here – it's getting stuck.'

'You mean the clutch?'

'The squishy gear one. Whatever it's called.'

'See you in an hour or so,' I said. 'Drive ... better.'

I stepped out of her car, feeling instantly safer, and strolled across the road. The tall building, number forty-three Sandy Street, looked like an office block. But I double-checked the address – definitely the right place. Inside there was a narrow corridor and then some steep steps – it was silent. The air swirled with incense smoke, a bit like Amy's room smells sometimes.

The wooden stairs creaked under my feet and, at the top, I went through another door and into a small reception area. Some gentle background music was playing – a twinkly harp mixed with the sound of waves. It was probably meant to be relaxing.

'Hi there,' I said to the woman behind the desk. 'I have an appointment.'

'Who are you?' she asked.

I thought of a head in a jar and then said my name.

'Go on through.' She pointed her thumb over her shoulder.

Approaching a tall wooden door with a shiny bronze handle and a window, I noticed the name Dr

Vladovski printed on the frosted glass. I pushed it open. Inside, sitting cross-legged in the middle of his desk, a man was making a strange humming noise. He was wearing a brown jacket, smart trousers and had a completely bald head. As he was facing away from me, I coughed to get his attention. Lifting his knees, he spun round on the desk, knocking some paper on to the floor in the process. He had glasses with perfectly round lenses, a waistcoat and a huge beard, a grey bush – it looked like his face was on the wrong way, all his hair on the bottom instead of the top.

'Oh yes, hello, I am Niko Vladovski,' he said in a strong Russian accent. He kicked his feet forwards and leapt off the desk. 'Very good welcome to you.'

'Hi. Uh, thanks.'

He stepped past and closed the door. 'Come, come inside. You come to see Vladovski for therapy?'

'Yeah, but, I dunno if I, like, need it or whatever.'

'Well, let's have a little talk time and then we can— Hey, it's you.' He pointed, his face lighting up, his beard stretching with excitement. '*Put a little honey on a puffy wheaty puff-puff,*' he sang. '*Hey, puff-puff, wheaty puff puff. Yum-yum puff-puff, tasty-tasty-tasty time.*'

'Hmm, close enough.' I sighed.

Vladovski was singing the incredibly popular, catchy jingle from an advert I was in last year and he was getting it quite wrong. I played the part of a kid eating Puff Puff Wheat Puffs and had to sing a little song at the end. If I had known that *everyone* in the country would see and remember the advert, I probably would have said no. I can't tell you how often someone shouts '*Yum-yum puff-puff*' at me in the street. And at school it's non-stop – even the teachers do jokes from time to time. I can't wait to be famous for something better than that.

'I love this commercial, my friend,' Vladovski said. 'We do not have delicious cereal like Puff Puff Wheat Puffs in old country. In my village we eat only sawdust and water from very brown pond.'

'Sounds horrible.'

'It was pretty bad, but they say wood porridge, it put hair on chest. Anyway, you make yourself comfortable. Sit on whichever chair you like.'

There were three chairs. A blue one, a red one and then a brown sofa. I felt like even this choice would say something about me.

'So you're a hypnotherapist?' I asked, stepping towards the sofa on the other side of the room.

'Yes, among other things. I like to focus on the mindfulness.'

I wandered across his strange office, noticing all his unusual books – many were leather-bound with oriental-style words on their spine – and on the wall was a black and white photo of him standing next to a huge bear.

'Hey, cool bear,' I said, looking over my shoulder.

'Ah, yes.' He strode up behind me. 'This is my old partner. We had circus show. I ride on his back, we jump through fire hoops, swing from rope – very good fun times.'

'That sort of sounds quite cruel . . .'

'Cruel? No. Bear, he likes it. We feed him the tuna legs and he perform very nice.'

'Strange career change? Circus trainer to therapist?'

'Ah, well, circus closed down after my bear, he, he go crazy and bite off my hand.' Vladovski held up his arm – only then did I notice he had a hook coming from his left sleeve.

'Wow.'

'But I forgive him. Many years ago now ...' He stroked his beard and sighed at his memories. 'Please, sit, sit. Let Vladovski fix your mind. What is this problem? You need to quit gambling? Smoking?'

'I'm eleven.' I sat back into the sofa.

'Then you really should not be gambling and smoking. You did right thing to come to Vladovski.'

I explained that I just got nervous, normal stage fright, and he said it was easy to sort out.

'Two sessions, maybe three, you never feel scared again,' he said. 'So, to start, you must close your eyes and take a long, slow, deep breath in through your nose and gently out through your mouth ...'

An hour later, right there in that room, it happened. The strangest experience of my entire life.

The doctor got me to lie down on the sofa and imagine I had floated out of my body and gone off to next week's audition. He told me to create a vivid image in my mind of what it would be like – the smells, the sounds, the fear I might feel. I pictured it so clearly, it felt real – or at least as real as a dream. Then he told me to imagine I was confident – like a bright, tall, beaming film of the best acting I'd ever done.

Once we'd finished all this, he counted down from ten and said that, when he gets to one, I should wake up and be 'back in room'.

'. . . four, three, two and . . . one.'

Slowly I opened my eyes and saw the office. The books. The desk. The empty blue chair. But something was wrong. Glancing down, I could see a brown blazer and a shiny silver hook instead of my left hand. There was a notepad on my lap – or *his* lap – my name was at the top and I read the words 'Money concerns?', 'Pet dog?' and 'Identity issues (understandable)?'. He'd also drawn a small doodle in the corner of the page – a little stickman with three eyes, one in the centre of his head.

And there, across the room, I saw *myself*, Chester Parsons, lying on the sofa with my eyes shut tight. I was . . . I was someone else now. I was Dr Vladovski.

Remember when I said auditions were the scariest things of all time? Well, I was wrong.

Chapter 2

Furry Sticks

Right, so we just need to run through some basics about consciousness before we go any further with the story. Ever heard of meditation? Probably. Ever tried it? Probably not.

Well, it's super simple and actually pretty amazing. All you do is sit somewhere quiet and close your eyes. Then you breathe in through your nose and slowly out through your mouth. Do that like, I don't know, ten times or whatever. Concentrate on your breathing, on how it sounds, how it feels. Be aware of your chest lifting and falling. Maybe your nose whistles slightly. Maybe not. Either way. Notice it. Then concentrate on your body – what can you feel? Think about every single thing touching it. Your clothes. Maybe your hands are touching each other. What does that feel like? Can you feel the ground? Sounds too, be aware of them. What can you hear?

Then, and this is where it gets interesting, pay attention to your *thoughts*.

The most amazing part of this mindfulness business is that it's so simple and so obvious. All you do is *look* at your own thoughts.

That's it.

Just notice what's happening in your head.

Close your eyes and just *think*. Do it. What the hell is going on in there? Just random thoughts coming and going. Thinking is easy, you've been doing it your whole life. But I tell you what isn't easy – *not thinking*. In fact, it's impossible. I bet you're thinking, 'Hey, I could stop thinking'. Give it a go. I will give you a million pounds if you can close your eyes and stop thinking for one minute. It might be that you're thinking and you haven't even noticed. But pay attention and you'll see that your mind is *constantly running*. If you think you've cracked it, if you think your mind is blank, you are probably thinking about how good you are at not thinking. Which is thinking. That or you're dead. If you're dead then this exercise is not for you.

I didn't know any of this jazzy consciousness stuff until Vladovski, the Russian hypnotherapist and ex-circus bear trainer, taught me. He said, 'You can no more stop your brain than you can stop your heart.'

But, of course, I'm getting distracted again, so let's go back to number forty-three Sandy Street, back to Dr Vladovski's office, back to the moment I woke up in *his* mind instead of my own.

'You can open your eyes now, Chester,' I said, in a Russian accent.

Then, with a strange whooshing noise that reminded me of fast wind in a storm, my vision went blurry, foggy and . . . and I jolted.

Darkness.

I was lying down on a sofa. I checked with one eye, then both. And when I sat up and looked, I saw the office. I saw Dr Vladovski.

'Whoa,' I said, touching my own arms and legs. 'That was crazy.'

'You like this?' the bald doctor asked. 'You feel confident to go to audition now?'

'Um … yeah … did … What *exactly* did you do to me?'

'I did nothing to you, Chester. Only *you* can make long-term changes to your mind.'

'Right. Sure. It's just …'

I wanted to tell him what had happened, I wanted to explain the experience, but I felt silly, I thought he might laugh. Or, worse, decide I was insane and call whoever you call in that situation.

Dr Vladovski placed the notepad and his glasses on the table by his side. 'You come back on Tuesday, we do a little more.'

'Sure,' I said, standing up.

Obviously it had just been in my imagination, I thought. It's not actually possible to put your consciousness in someone else's brain. It's not actually possible to *become* someone else. I *was* being silly. I was smart enough to know that it must have just been an illusion, like a dream.

But as I stepped towards the door, I glanced down

at Vladovski's notepad. The notes were familiar and so was the small three-eyed stickman doodle in the top right-hand corner. My eyes were as wide as they'd ever been as I walked outside and felt the bright summer sun on my skin.

At dinner, Amy was talking fast about her YouTube channel, about subscribers or something like that – I wasn't really listening.

'It used to go up by a thousand or so a month,' she was saying to Mum. 'But recently it's slowed right down. I just don't understand what I'm doing wrong.'

'Maybe you've got to keep it fresh,' Mum said. 'Review different things? What would you give dinner?'

'I'd say nine point five.' Amy smiled. 'Ten for the chicken, but the vegetables could be firmer.'

'Well, you can cook tomorrow.'

'I just *know* Brian will ask about numbers.'

'As long as he's watched some of your videos, I'm sure they'll be interested in working with you.'

'I hope so.' Amy's knife and fork clinked on her plate as she finished. She took a long swig of water.

'You're very quiet, Chester,' Mum said.

'Huh?' I turned my head but not my eyes. 'Oh yeah, sure.'

'Tell me more about your session with Dr Vladovski. How did it go, what did you learn?'

'Um, good.' I stared at the broccoli on my plate, poking it a few times with my fork. 'Mindfulness.'

'Oh, that's interesting, I was ...' She carried on talking, but I realised I wasn't paying attention.

Right. What am I thinking? That's what Dr Vladovski said I should say to myself. This would help me notice my thoughts.

What *was* I thinking?

About what happened, about the notepad that proved it *was* real. There was no other way I could have seen those notes and that doodle other than through the doctor's eyes. I had become him. I had ... I don't know. I had been *in* his mind. Or in his body. Just like I am in *my* body now.

So the next question was: could I do it again?

22

After we'd cleared all the plates away and wiped the table, Amy went upstairs to record a video. I paced up and down my bedroom, which is next door to hers, trying to work out a way of testing it. How had it happened? I was relaxed and I imagined *myself* leaving my body (whatever 'myself' actually is). Then, when I came back, I must have missed *my* body and ended up in Vladovski's. But to get back into my own body I just looked at myself and, click, it happened.

Maybe seeing was the key – they say the eyes are the window to the soul after all. Right, so I needed a test subject.

'Hey guys, welcome to *Amy Reviews*,' I heard Amy say. 'Today I'm going to cover a few of my favourites from this summer – I'll do a top five and a bottom five next week.'

I stepped into the hall – sneaky, quiet. Amy's door was open a little bit – I could see her sitting at her desk, in front of her computer, talking into the webcam. She's got this YouTube channel, called *Amy Reviews*, where she chats about stuff – films, books, songs, chocolate bars, make-up, literally anything. Then she scores it out of ten and judges them on the 'Amy Scale'. It's quite a good idea I guess and she's got thousands of subscribers.

But I didn't care about all that. All I cared about was whether I could get into her mind. So I sat carefully on the carpet outside her room and pushed the door open a tiny bit more. She was halfway through listing her favourite movies of the year when I began. I stared at the back of her head, frowning, rubbing my temples with two fingers – I don't know why, it just felt like the right thing to do. I breathed slowly, calmly, and imagined I was leaving my body, floating through the air and rushing into her brain. After straining and even nodding my head forwards, as though I was trying to throw off a hat, I realised how crazy I must have looked.

Maybe I am crazy?

No. Not crazy. Keep trying.

I sat there for about ten minutes doing this. I was about to give up but, for some reason, Amy turned to look over her shoulder. Maybe she could feel me watching her – I don't know.

The second we made eye contact it happened again. That strange zipping wind noise and then I was looking back at myself sitting on the carpet in the hall. My eyes were closed, I was just sitting there cross-legged outside her room – to be fair, from her point of view, it *did* look weird.

'Chester, what the hell are you doing?' I said in her voice as I strode across her bedroom and slammed the door in my own face.

Bang. I gasped and was back in my body.

I decided that this ... Well, I didn't really know what to call it. Superpower? Ability? Curse? Skill? Whatever. Whatever *this* was, it was something I wanted to get better at.

So over that weekend, I practised and practised. On Sunday I went into town and tried it on strangers. I leapt into the mind of a street sweeper, a policeman – I even spent ten seconds in the body of an ice-cream seller. I'd never seen the inside of an ice-cream van – not as exciting as you might imagine.

In the park I'd been leaping from person to person for about an hour. I sat on a bench near the fence so

I could see everyone. I would look across the grass and paths, through the hazy sunlight, past the tree shadows swaying on the ground – a few butterflies and tiny bugs like living dust in the beams of yellow – and select my next target.

I glanced at some kids playing football – zip-whoosh, I'm kicking a ball. From him I would look at a woman pushing a pram, hiss-whistle, I'm in her mind. Then I might dart across the park in a blink and I'm that guy with dreadlocks riding a BMX.

I rode around in a circle watching myself do some tricks, then cycled past a kid with brown hair sitting on a bench with his eyes shut – but before I could think it was strange, I opened my eyes and I was Chester Parsons again.

'*Yum-yum puff-puff,*' someone shouted. I didn't even care.

During these experiments it had felt like I was just watching through someone else's eyes. Like a passenger in their body. But then I got to wondering – what if I could *control* people too, that might be fun. I scanned the sunny park for a target. Plenty to choose from, but – *there* – that guy. A shrieking blink and I was in his body.

Then I decided he should buy some candyfloss, so I strode confidently, easily, to the ice-cream van and pointed at a sugary bush hanging in a bag from the ceiling. It reminded me of Vladovski's beard but, you know, bright pink. I pushed my hand into his pocket (at this point I felt like I was doing something wrong – was this pickpocketing?). I looked down – in the guy's hand, my hand, whoever's hand, there was a pound coin. I placed it on the metal counter. Clink. Done.

Sitting on a bench, I was literally beside myself with joy as I began eating the candyfloss. I could *taste* it. But then, suddenly, it all went weird. Something was building. Something awful. I felt nauseous, dizzy and ... Oh no, no – don't be sick. Before I puked, I looked to my left and flashed back into my own body. There he was, the guy I was just driving, staring right into my eyes. He was incredibly pale – he held a fist to his mouth, took a deep breath, and frowned at the pink bundle of candyfloss on the end of the stick in his hand. Then he stood, dropped it in the bin and rushed out of the park. Maybe he didn't like candyfloss, I thought. Or maybe having your brain invaded feels horrible?

One more and then I'd go home. I searched for another victim.

No, victim's the wrong word. That sounds bad. Is this an OK thing to do? Or is it like reading someone's diary or something? Snooping through their room? Worse maybe? Who knows, who cares, it was way too much fun. (I often have thoughts like this whenever I do something I know is wrong. But then another part of me thinks, 'Ah, so what, just do it.' This has got me in plenty of trouble. Maybe I should listen more to the first voice . . .?)

In the middle of the park there was a small play area – kids on swings, toddlers going up and down the slide, some dodgy-looking teenagers making the roundabout go ridiculously fast. But on the other side, sitting in a shadow under a tree, I spotted my final role of the day – a kid around my age with a puppy.

I'd *love* a puppy, I thought, as I took a deep breath in and felt my consciousness drift up and flow like an electrical signal across the park.

But, at the last moment, his dog leapt into the air, trying to grab a butterfly, and then everything looked completely wrong. I was too low, all the colours of the park were gone, my vision was blurry, black and white, like watching a really old TV underwater. But everything smelled *incredible* – the grass, the candyfloss in the bin a hundred metres away, that woman's perfume, the leaves, the daisies, my owner's shampoo.

I ran in a circle, the world bouncing and rolling as I chased a furry stick of some kind. Man, I wanted that furry stick more than I'd ever wanted anything in my entire life. I would *kill* for that stick – why can't I catch it? It's, always, just, out, of, reach.

Hang on. I stopped. Licked my paw. That's not a stick, that's my tail. Ha ha, I'm so stupid.

'Sit. Ruby, sit.'

Who said that? Sit? Sit where? Sit why?

Wait. Stop. What's that? Hotdog. There's a hotdog here. Somewhere in this park someone is eating a hotdog. That is a fact. Mustard. Ketchup.

Hang on. Fried onions too. Sweet baby—

Where is that? Where *is* that hotdog? I would do—

There's that furry stick again, come here, you little – stay *still*, you horrible waggly—

Wait.

A new smell. Something that must DIE. *Another dog*. It's looking at me. It wants to fight. I will ruin you, doggo, I will destroy you. Yeah, keep walking, keep walking.

'Ruby, *sit*!'

Look, kid, I'm clearly not in the business of following orders, now share that sandwich and we might be able to come to some sort of—

HANG ON.

I'm a dog?

Chapter 3

Webcam Squirrel or, I don't know, the Sword of Sugar? Chapter titles are hard

When I realised I had accidentally put my consciousness in the mind of a dog, I panicked. You know in a dream when something horrible happens and you go, 'Oh no, wait, this is a dream,' and kick your legs out and then wake up? Well, it felt a bit like that. But instead of waking up, I transferred back into my own body.

Across the park, I saw the dog – a fluffy young Labrador called Ruby, staring back at me. Then it carried on chasing its tail. The reason I had aimed for the owner was simple – I wanted to know what it felt like to have a puppy again. Even if it was just for a few seconds.

We used to have a dog, Dandelion, until a couple of years ago when she ran away. *Someone* left the side gate open. I say someone – it was me. Or, at least, Mum and Amy believe it was me. I was last in the garden but I was *so sure* I closed the gate. But I guess my memory isn't quite as strong as the evidence. Gate open. Dog gone.

Two days later, a policeman came and gave Mum the collar and said she'd been hit by a car. I'll be honest, it messed me up. I cried. Not just a few sniffs and a watery eye. Actual crying. Not only because Dandelion was dead, but because it was all my fault.

Now I always check the gate three times before I leave the garden, even though we don't have any pets to escape.

Smiling one last time at that puppy, I headed for the park's exit.

A part of me felt I should keep this ability secret – I don't know why, but that's what people do, isn't it? Not tell anyone and then fight crime or whatever?

Well, I was having none of that. So I ran home and told Amy.

Out of breath, I burst into her room without knocking, then worried for a moment because this usually makes her extremely angry. But she was smiling, almost crying with happiness. She looked like she'd won the lottery or something. She closed a window on her laptop and spun in her swivel chair to face me.

'Amy, listen, something weird is happening.'

'Chester, I have *the best* news.'

'Sure, but listen, I can go into people's minds. Dogs too. It's crazy, I—'

'That's great, Chester, well done,' she said, but I could tell she hadn't really listened. 'Now sit down.'

I perched on her bed, which had white fairy lights wrapped around the metal frame, even though it wasn't Christmas, and a completely ridiculous amount of cushions and pillows. No one needs that many cushions.

'I just had a video call with Brian from Red Rose Pictures.'

'Um, OK? Who's that?' I knew I had to listen to her news before I told her mine.

'Brian Lipton is a television producer.' She grabbed me by the shoulders. 'He saw some of *Amy Reviews* and got in touch. They want me to present a new show. A TV show, Chester. They want *me* to be a presenter. Can you imagine what that'll do to my profile? The subscribers, the followers, the sheer numbers! They've invited me to their head office for a meeting. I have to tell Mum.' She stood.

'This is good news,' I said. 'But, please, I need you to listen to me.'

She sat back down and I explained everything. The whole situation. And I could tell she had heard this time because she was frowning and scrunching up her lip.

When I finished, she seemed angry.

'Chester, have you been taking drugs?!'

'What? No.'

'I'm telling Mum. You're *eleven*. Where did you get it?'

'I swear it's true. I've done it to you.'

'Birds go tweet, cows go moo.' (Amy is good at the rhyming game.)

'I . . . no,' I said. 'Not now. I saw myself through *your eyes* – remember, when I was staring at you from the hall? You slammed the door.'

'Is this some kind of prank – are you secretly filming this?' She looked around for a camera and touched her hair.

'No.'

'Fine . . . Prove it. Jump into the mind of . . .' She glanced around the room again, then turned to the window. '. . . *that* squirrel. Right there, in the tree, see him? Get that squirrel to come and dance on my desk.'

I stood and pulled her white curtain to the side. 'Well, I've never done it on a squirrel, I don't know if—'

'How convenient. Look, can we wrap this up? I—'

'All right, wait,' I said, sitting on the bed and relaxing.

The squirrel hopped fast along the branch, then spiralled up the tree and paused on the corner of a broken twig. I stared into its brown eyes, breathed, and felt that weird feeling again. When I blinked, I arrived in the creature's tiny little mind.

At first it was hard to control my new body – it felt too light. I looked down. My furry hands were gripping the rough bark and all I wanted to do was climb and eat nuts. *Man, nuts are so awesome. Hazelnuts, crunchy little acorns, sesame crackers, nibble, nibble, yum, yum, yum – no, concentrate.* To my left I spotted the open window. Amy was glancing from the squirrel (me) to Chester (also me), her eyebrows lifted high and her arms folded tight.

I ran to the end of the branch, which tilted and swayed in the breeze. Then, lining myself up, I leapt and grabbed the windowsill. Scrabbling up with my hind legs, I could hear my claws scratching the bricks until, with a final jump, I was inside. I waved my tail, stared at Amy and tried to smile. But I don't think squirrels *can* smile, so I probably just showed my teeth. Might have even hissed. It must have looked scary because Amy stepped back and grabbed a book to defend herself – not sure what she thought might happen.

'Chester, it's in the room.'

Squirrel me leapt down on to the carpet then up on to her bed, clambering through the warm, glowing fairy lights. Finally, I jumped on to her desk, ran around in a few circles, stood up straight and made a squeaky chirping noise – I was trying to say 'Ta-da', but squirrels' vocal chords are *weak*.

'Uh, Amy.' A posh voice echoed from her laptop. The sound startled me and, with a twitch, I was back in my body. In a panic the grey squirrel darted across the desk, knocking over a pot of pens, then dived for the window and was gone.

Amy stared at me as she approached her computer. She clicked her video call open and a man appeared in the centre of the screen. He was wearing a suit and a pearly white smile.

'Yah, OK,' he said. 'I just wanted to say, you didn't disconnect the call.'

'Did you hear all that?' I asked.

'Every word. Chester, come forward so I can get a look at you,' the man said. I stood in front of the screen. Me and Amy side by side in one window, the suited man in the other. 'Yah, OK. Handsome. Good teeth. Nice face. My name's Brian Lipton, pleased to meet you.'

'Uh, hi,' I said. This man had seen the entire squirrel stunt through Amy's webcam. For some reason I felt embarrassed.

'How's your schedule looking today? Can we do lunch?'

This Brian Lipton guy was a TV producer, as Amy had said. Which, for people not involved in showbiz, is basically someone who makes TV shows. An hour later he was ringing our doorbell and shaking hands with Mum in the hallway.

'Mrs Parsons,' he said. 'And Amy, darling.' He greeted her too. 'And the man of the house, Chesto.' Brian held his fists like a boxer and pretended to punch me on the chin. Then he yelled with laughter and rubbed my shoulder. 'I'm just playing,' he shouted.

I liked him – he was clearly . . . not quite stupid, but simple, dim, in a fun way. Plus he had sort of orange skin from fake tan which made him easy to laugh at. Mum said he was 'charming'.

Before he arrived, we had to explain everything to her as well. At first I think she didn't really get it – like when I show her something on her laptop and she nods and says, 'Oh yes, I understand.' Although obviously she doesn't.

Once we looked at our house on Google Street View and she asked if it was a live feed. I just stared at her and slowly shook my head.

We all sat at the kitchen table. Mum started to make coffee and Brian removed a pen from his top pocket, then clicked open his briefcase.

'Yah, riiiight, yah, OK,' he said. 'You two, Chester and Amy, Amy and Chester.' He framed us with his fingers and thumbs. 'A reality show, both your talents, Amy bringing that charisma we love online, presenting Chester's abilities, maybe some aerobatics – get a performing squirrel and— Is it just squirrels, or . . .?'

'I dunno really, this is quite new,' I said. 'People, dogs, squirrels so far. Not sure of the risks so . . .'

'Yah, yah, yah, no, no. Great. Just great. Whatever you did, whether that's a magic trick, or CGI, or whatever, it was fantastic. Studio will love it. This will sell. It will sell big.'

'How big?' Amy asked.

'Hard to say, hard to say. How's fifty K each sound? Right off the bat. As a sign of goodwill, an advance for the contract?'

'You mean fifty thousand pounds?' Amy said, making double sure, looking at me with wide eyes.

'Right, this is nice and all,' I said. 'But I'm not really sure I want to be the star of a reality show. Don't know if Amy mentioned, but I'm actually an actor and—'

'Oh, Chest-o, OK, yah, I'm reading you loud and clear. It will be tasteful, classy. Who's your agent?'

'David Brenden.'

'Davey B?! Lovely chap.'

'Also, it might conflict with a film I've got coming up,' I said.

'Riiight. Yah. Sure. Put the acting on the back burner for now. Get your name in lights, then the world is your oyster.' He pointed at me with his finger, winked and clicked it as though it was a gun. 'Shall I tell the studio we're greenlighting this?'

'I mean … this is all happening so quickly. Maybe

you should just stick with the original plan, get Amy to do a show and leave me out of it.'

'Chester,' Amy whispered through clenched teeth. 'Can I have a word?'

She dragged me into the hall.

'I don't want to be famous for this – I don't even know what *this* is,' I said.

'Listen to me,' Amy said. 'We need the money. You're too young to understand, but why do you think Mum has been so quiet and sad recently? Work has made her redundant. She has no job. If we don't get some cash soon we're going to have to sell the house.'

I actually *did* understand this. Mum tried her best to keep our money issues a secret, but it's fairly obvious. I know what those red bank letters in the post mean. This was another reason why *Sword of Steel and Stone* was so exciting. Sure, I have earned quite a lot of money from adverts – Puff Puff Wheat Puffs was well paid – but a main part in a big blockbuster movie like that? It would sort everything.

'I'm not too young to understand,' I said.

'*Please*, do the show. They won't hire me without you. Don't ruin this.'

'Amy,' I whispered, 'I am going to be in the *Sword of Steel and Stone* movie. I am an actor. Not a freak. Not a famous ... squirrel charmer. I'm sorry, but the answer is no.'

After the meeting, Brian seemed disappointed – he said we should give it some thought and call him with a final answer. But when I visited Vladovski, I felt sure I had already done the right thing.

'Ah, Chester,' the doctor said as I arrived. 'Sit, sit.'

'I need to tell you something.' I went to the sofa. He sat on the red chair opposite. 'Last week, when you hypnotised me ...'

I told him the whole story so far. He frowned and nodded.

'I know it sounds insane,' I added.

'My job is not to judge, but you need to be aware of the risks.'

'Hang on. You ... believe me?'

'Of course.'

'Oh.' This was not the response I was expecting. I'd just told a therapist I could control people *and* wildlife with my mind. You'd *think* men in white coats would arrive. Maybe they were on their way. Maybe he had a secret button?

'You,' Vladovski said, 'are a Daahsuti . . .'

'A what?'

'In your language you'd say you're a mind jumper.'

'Sounds like a fancy hat.'

'You . . . you do something that takes others many years. You ever hear expression old soul? Well, you, my friend, are one of the oldest. But I . . . I mustn't . . . I cannot tell you more.'

'OK? So how does this . . . this mind jumping work?' I was relieved to hear it was a real thing – I wasn't crazy. Phew.

He hesitated for a few seconds. 'My . . . my teacher, guru, back in old country, he taught that it is like swimming in underwater cave,' he said. 'Along ceiling of the cave, there are holes, places where you can come up and breathe. Conscious beings are like these air holes. When you leave your own body, you swim

43

in pure consciousness, then arrive in new mind. You understand?'

'Not really. But, I mean, can other people do this?'

'Yes.' Vladovski stroked his beard and tried to hide a smile.

'*You* can do it?'

He nodded. 'But you must understand, Chester, this is no game. You play with fire, you get burned.' He lifted his hook hand – whoa, I forgot about that thing.

'Wait. The bear – *that's* how you did your circus show?'

Vladovski nodded again. 'During Cold War, Russian KGB has mystic training camps – you know KGB?'

'Maybe . . . um . . .'

'KGB was Russian intelligence. You know, spies. With them, I learn this art. I lose myself. I learn who I am. But I leave KGB. Work for circus. But what I did – controlling the animals, making them perform, it can get you in a lot of trouble.'

'I'm not going near any bears.'

'Bear is dangerous, yes – it pull off head like piece of soft bread no problem. But this is not trouble I

44

speak of. For real trouble, you must look to the ancient order – the star swimmers.'

'What's that?'

'It ...' Vladovski seemed like he didn't want to explain. 'I can't ...'

'Tell me,' I said.

'It ... it is an organisation, many hundreds of years old. They meditate in cave, in snow. You know men in robes who say, "Ommm, ommm, ding, ding, ding, ommm". They police the ancient practices, they keep it secret.'

'Are they ... cool? I mean, they sound cool.'

'No,' Vladovski said, shocked that I would even ask. 'They are more dangerous than most angry bear you ever see. This is why you *must* resist urge to jump from mind to mind. Do not take this path. You concentrate *only* on being best actor.'

'Not a problem. I'm done with it. Acting all the way.'

'This is good. I know men who leave themselves too long, get lost, you see? You wander too far from home and you might forget way back ...'

*

The morning of the final *Sword of Steel and Stone* audition was a beautiful one. The sun was shining, birds were chirping in the trees, butterflies were in the air – it looked like a movie. Me, I was calm, I was collected. I was Chester Parsons, the best actor of his generation. Confident, filled with all the strength and power Dr Vladovski had taught me. Nervous? Ha. Not even slightly.

The casting people were sitting behind a table when I read my lines. The script they'd given me to perform was a really big scene from the film. I knew what they wanted. They wanted emotion. And man did I deliver.

At the end of the scene I fell to my knees. 'Ah!' I yelled, clutching my heart (in this part of the script I had just been shot with an arrow). I rolled on to my back on the floor and pretended I was dying. My performance was incredible. 'Tell them what happened here,' I whispered. 'Tell them that ... tell them ... tell them that I tried ...' And then, with a final breath, I was dead.

My eyes were closed but I could hear the applause. When I looked, all the casting people, the director, the producer, even the woman who was just there making coffee, were on their feet, clapping. One of them wiped away a tear.

The feeling I had when I left that studio was probably the best in my life. I felt I might fly. I saw Amy's lovely little car waiting for me – I actually danced across the car park, shuffling, clicking my fingers, pointing at her as I approached.

'Well, good afternoon there,' I said, my face aching from my smile. 'How are you on this fine day?'

'Go well?'

'I aced it. I think it was the best acting I've ever done. I got a standing ovation.'

'So the part's yours?'

'I've never been so sure of anything.' I tilted my head back and sighed. If Amy wasn't looking at me, I might have even cried tears of joy. 'Dave will call later with the details.'

Mum was over the moon when I told her how well it went. She hugged me and said I was talented. I was actually *excited* about going back to school – in fact, I was excited about everything.

That evening I was in the living room, my feet were on the coffee table and my heart was still warm and fuzzy. Then, with a loud buzz, my phone moved across the sofa cushion by my side. It was Dave, my agent, who got me the audition in the first place.

Here we go, I thought, fingers and toes wiggling in excitement. I pressed answer. 'Dave!' I said.

'You all right, Chester?'

'Best day of my life probably.'

'Ah ... well, that's why I was calling. They gave the part to the other guy. Sorry, kid.'

'That's great news, man,' I said, still smiling. 'Did they say when filming would— Wait, what?'

'Couple of notes here. You seemed too calm – they said you were almost too good. You'd lost your vulnerability.'

'*Too good*? What? No. *No.*'

'You can't win 'em all, bud.'

'But ... but ...' It felt like the world was falling. I could have been sick. 'But ... I've told everyone at school I've got the part.'

'Well, September's going to suck for you then.'

'I . . . I was so sure.'

'Listen, Chester, it's not a big deal. Take it on the chin. Look, I've got to go. Speak soon.'

The phone went silent against my ear.

Mum and Amy burst into the living room. They had a cake. Amy set off a party popper.

I had died and gone to hell.

'I . . . I didn't get the part,' I said, staring at the wall.

Mum tutted and looked sad as she set the cake on the table. It had a sword made of icing sticking out the top.

But Amy? She frowned and then grinned. 'So . . . that means . . . we *can* do the show?' She dived on to the sofa and hugged me. 'This is the best bad news of all time. I'll call Brian. Remember, Chester, everything happens for a reason.'

Chapter 4

The Worst Thing of All Time

I suppose I should tell you when everything went wrong. Things were quite bad already and, at the time, I honestly thought they couldn't get any worse. Which is hilarious now I think about it. But, seriously, this next part of the story includes probably the worst thing that could ever happen. If I had to score it on the Amy Scale, it'd get minus a million.

It happened at the zoo.

A week after my brutal, crushing rejection, we started filming *Amy and Chester*. I still wasn't at all keen on the idea, but Amy was right – we needed the money.

'As you grow older,' Vladovski had said during our

last session, 'you will find it astonishing what people are willing to do for money.'

I decided not to tell him that I hadn't got the *Sword of Steel and Stone* part and, for obvious reasons, didn't mention that I was, instead, starring in a TV show all about my mind-jumping abilities. Somehow, I thought he wouldn't approve. I did *try* and explain his warnings to Brian and Amy – about the risks, about that 'ancient order' of mystic mind jumpers. But they just laughed – right in my face. It did sound pretty far-fetched when I said it out loud.

Yeah, sure, I thought, it'll probably be fine. (There's that voice again.)

Brian and a cameraman came to the house and, once Mum had signed a couple of contracts and listened to some boring legal chat, they hit record and we were rolling. They also gave me and Amy a small handheld camera each to film diary pieces in our spare time. There was no real plan at first – it was, as Brian said, a reality show.

'Just be your wonderful selves,' he explained. 'Try and act as though the camera isn't even here.'

But, pretty quickly, Brian was telling us what to do. Apparently, sitting around watching TV and being normal isn't *actually* that interesting. Soon enough, the show was just me doing funny things to people and animals.

Even though I was the star, Amy loved every minute of it.

Obviously she's my sister, so I would be sad if she died probably, but I do sort of feel like she's a loser. Lots of people think she's cool because she *acts* cool on her videos and has nice hair and wears expensive clothes or whatever, but she's just ... I don't know. It's like she cares way too much what other people think. Like, she would do literally anything to make people like her. Anything. If eating live kittens became fashionable, she'd grab the nearest one and take a massive furry bite out of it. She wouldn't even hesitate.

Also, she starts all her videos with the words 'Hey guys' and a wave. Gah. That annoys me so much. Because she's just *copying* other people. It's like she's acting.

When she was younger and we used to play

together, she was Just Amy. I knew her. Hey, look, that's Amy – she's all right. But as she got older and started filming herself and taking pictures of her lunch and basically posting *everything* online, she changed. Her personality split in two.

So there would be the real Amy (Just Amy), and the Amy that she becomes on camera (Loser Amy). One is my sister and she's fairly cool. The other is embarrassing and I hate her and I hope she falls down some stone stairs. Maybe that's a bit much but you get my point.

The reason I bring all this up is because that chirpy 'Hey guys' had found its way into this stupid, pointless show we were making. Every scene would start with Amy looking at the camera and presenting the situation.

'Hey guys, we're here at the park today . . .'

Hey guys, look, wow, Chester can be a dog. Hey look, wow, he can be a badger. Hey look, wow, he can be a horse. Hey look, wow, his soul is dead. Hey look, wow, he's the saddest person of all time.

They posted a couple of videos on YouTube straight

away – one where Amy explained that I was a mind jumper – and then I leapt into the body of various animals they brought to the house especially. A dog, a mouse, a bat for some reason. The video was edited to a cool song and, within hours, Brian said it was 'Trending worldwide, darlings.' Because that's the kind of stuff he says.

You might think all this would be awesome, but you'd be wrong. It wasn't fun any more. It was ridiculous. I felt like a clown. Dancing about in the body of animals just for a few million YouTube hits and a bit (all right, a *lot*) of money. Amazing, really, how something as incredible as mind jumping gets boring once you turn it into a cheap trick.

At least when I was controlling animals I was distracted. This is the strange thing about mind jumping. When you're in a person, it's quite straightforward – it feels pretty much the same as normal, except obviously you're looking through different eyes, listening through different ears and so on. But with an animal, you get a mix of feelings. Like, when I was a mouse, I had this intense fear of cats, which didn't wear off for ages after I returned to my body. Imagine a cat the size of a house, like a T-Rex, hunting you and toying with you and trying to rip you to pieces and stuff – for *fun*. If that doesn't scare you then you're not imagining it properly.

Anyway, in total there were six episodes in the first series. We watched them all once they had been edited – to be fair, some of it *was* funny. There was a great bit when I was in a swan running through a busy shopping centre, causing absolute feathery carnage, screeching at people and flapping my wings, knocking over shelves and bins. I chased one guy until he cried. That was a good day, I enjoyed that. But once you'd seen one episode, you'd seen them all.

Either way, the first series aired and, as predicted, we were famous. Yay. Everyone knew me as the kid who could control animals.

And yet, even then, people *still* shouted '*Yum-yum puff-puff*' at me. I reckon, when I die, that'll be carved into my gravestone.

Here lies Chester Parsons, YUM-YUM PUFF-PUFF.

I don't even like Puff Puff Wheat Puffs – we got them for free for a year after the advert and they make me sick. Taste like sugary bits of floor.

Once *Amy and Chester* was popular, we went on a few talk shows together. We were even on the morning news. This was more her thing than mine, so I let her do most of the talking. These interviews were always the same. The presenter would ask some general questions, about our fame, about the show, about the weather, whatever, and then they would say, 'Maybe Chester could demonstrate it now?' As if they just thought of that. Oh, while you're here – that's a good idea. Obviously that was the plan all along. That's why you invited me. Wheel out ya tortoise, let's get it done.

I did all this stuff with a smile though – I was professional about it. I'm good at pretending I'm enjoying myself – after all, I'm an actor (remember?).

You're probably thinking I was being ungrateful. You're probably thinking, hey, now *Amy and Chester* has finished, I could pick up where I left off – carry on acting.

But no. Wrong again.

You see, the contract was for *two* series of the show – and there was already talk of more. There was a break from filming, which seemed to fly past in a mad frenzy. And before I knew it, Christmas had been and gone, the park was frosty, and series two was about to begin.

The minibus pulled into the huge empty car park on a cold Sunday afternoon. This series would start a bit differently – we were going to film everything 'on location'. Day one. Scene one. The zoo.

'Yah, riiight, OK,' Brian said. 'We've got the run of the whole place today. Studio's throwing big money at this season. So I want everyone at their best. Lots of teeth – Amy, remember the necklace has to be visible or the sponsorship deal is void.'

Brian's enthusiasm was in top gear. Last year he was producing a fun show about a couple of kids. *This* year he had a million-pound budget and had to keep his bosses happy.

We all stepped out of the minibus and on to the tarmac.

'Chest-o,' Brian said. 'I want to see that dazzling

smile of yours too.' He grabbed me in a soft, playful headlock, his puffy blue coat ruffled my hair.

'Get off,' I said, laughing.

He let me go. 'That's the one – what a money-maker.'

'I'll see you in court,' I said, neatening my collar.

I'll admit his joy was infectious. He was probably the one thing that made it all bearable. When someone is constantly positive, it does make people happy.

They let us film in the zoo over a bank holiday weekend, but we had to wait until the evening, after closing time. I guess they didn't want us freaking out the visitors. As series two was 'bigger and better in every way', there were going to be more exotic creatures, more excitement and more, Brian said, 'Zing-zing pow.' Whatever that means.

The Silent Cameraman set everything up and found a good location to film. Thinking back, I honestly don't remember being introduced to him – I'm sure he had a name and I'm sure he could speak. But he never did. He just filmed. Maybe it was so we would forget he was even there. Either way, Silent Cameraman was what we called him.

'Let your hair down, Chester,' Amy (Just Amy) said, checking her make-up in the minibus's wing mirror. 'I know you're only pretending to be happy – no one else can see it, but I can.'

'I'll try.'

'Just have fun – when this is over, we'll get paid more money than we can even imagine. Plus, how often do we get to hang out and just muck about together?'

I smiled. 'Yeah.'

Damn. Just Amy was right.

I remembered my mindfulness training – where all this started. I have to look at my thoughts.

Could I make this positive? Easily. I was at a zoo. I had been nearly every domestic animal. But lions, tigers, giraffes? This was all new. All right – I decided I would enjoy myself.

'OK, yah, listen up, guys,' Brian said. 'Let's get some quick shots of the car park. Then, quick intro from Amy, Chest-o gets cosy in the van, then get yourself into a bird – maybe one of these crows.' There were three big black birds pecking at some rubbish a little way from the minibus. One squawked. 'Then down on to Amy's shoulder. We'll get a GoPro fitted, then into the zoo for some freestyling, yeah? Great. Great. Let's roll.'

By now, mind jumping was as straightforward as riding a bike. Easy once you know how. I didn't even need to concentrate. I just looked at an animal and – zip-whoosh – I was controlling it.

I pecked a hole in a polystyrene cup with my long black beak, leapt a couple of times on the spot and turned to look at Amy. Then, with a jump and a few flaps of my wings, I flew up and landed on top of the minibus. I peered down through the sunroof and saw my body sleeping peacefully in a trance below. Always weird to look back at yourself.

'Hey guys . . .' Loser Amy said.

Brian strapped a small camera round my neck, which meant I could film quite literally a bird's-eye view of the zoo. Being some animals did get dull but, when it came to flying, that was *always* great fun. Every single time, it felt amazing. It felt effortless, like in a dream – I just pushed up into the air and watched the ground fall away beneath me.

I drifted and glided and turned over the entire zoo, seeing it from above like a map, all the fields, paths, the huge empty car park, the minibus now just a tiny white rectangle. Then falling, spiralling, the wind rushing through my feathers, I landed on top of a cage. From there I would jump down into an animal, do some tricks, prove I was in control, then look up at the crow, shoot back into it, and then up and away.

It must have been about 6 p.m. when I arrived at Tito's enclosure. Tito, the eleven-year-old silverback gorilla. The zoo seemed especially proud of him – he had a huge cage all to himself, with tyre swings and ropes and platforms. Then a little tunnel, which had windows along either side, led to another enclosure with all the other gorillas, and an indoor area to sleep and eat. That section of the zoo was called Gorilla Mountain. All the signs, the benches, even the bins had little pictures of gorillas and notes with key facts about them. Did you know ninety-eight per cent of gorilla DNA is the same as *Homo sapiens* DNA (which is humans)? Did you know gorillas are the largest primate? Did you know gorilla eggs are the strongest eggs in nature?

I may have misremembered some of those facts.

As always, I looked down into the cage, spotted the target, then whistled through the air and arrived in his mind. Being a gorilla was awesome. I danced and swung and leapt around the enclosure. I made all the classic ooo-ooo-aaah-aaah sounds. I ran towards the edge of the cage, my big arms swinging. Then I did some roly-polies and threw straw all over myself. They even got me to paint some pictures and take selfies on a phone – one with the whole crew behind me.

It was evening when we wrapped it up for the day – it was getting dark, cold. The crow I'd been using to travel around was still waiting at the top of the cage, so I tilted my huge hairy black head and looked at it. Off I go. Farewell, Tito. It's been a laugh.

But nothing happened.

Huffing, frowning, I tried again. Then I stepped a bit closer to the bird – I tried sitting, relaxing, lying on the ground, but I just couldn't get out of the gorilla.

'Come on, Chester,' Amy said from behind the viewing glass, tapping her watch.

I could see a worried look on Brian's face. But Silent

Cameraman was still filming me. I roared and hit my chest.

Just do it, I thought, grabbing my head and groaning. By now I was in a bad state – a mix of angry and terrified. Which is an odd combination. I let out my loudest roar yet, which echoed around the zoo. The startled crow flapped its wings and left nothing but a single feather falling down through the air towards me like a black leaf.

Panicked, I stared at Amy. Maybe I should go for a human host. That's it. I would leap into *her* mind (even though she told me never to do it again) then get back to my body that way. But I couldn't do that either. I was stuck. Trapped in a gorilla, of all places.

Right at this point, I totally lost it. I grabbed at the fence, used a stick to try and break the viewing glass, then bashed into it with my shoulder and my heavy fists. Brian opened the enclosure and started to say something, but I barged past, knocking Silent Cameraman off his feet. One of the zookeepers set off an alarm, shouted. I didn't care.

All I wanted was to get back to my own body – a

direct jump was the only way. Nothing else mattered. Not the show. Not the fact that a gorilla was on the loose. Nothing.

I climbed the perimeter fence easily, then thundered on all fours straight into the car park, straight to the minibus, straight to the side. I ripped open the door, literally pulling off the handle and flinging it over my shoulder. Then, with a deep grumbling groan, I started to breathe faster and faster. My eyes wide and scared as they searched the empty seats.

My body was gone.

Chapter 5

The Naked Gorilla

Hey, remember earlier when we were talking about consciousness and I told you to look at your own thoughts? Did you do it? Notice anything strange? For me, it was like realising I'd been driving around for years and had never even spotted the car. The weirdest part though is that no one's actually steering.

That thing you say is 'you', like, the little person in your brain, is actually a thought itself. When you go looking for 'you', it usually disappears. It's difficult to explain and some people try for decades to realise this, so don't feel bad if you don't figure it out straight away.

Also, I was surprised by how thoughts actually happen. Close your eyes and have a look inside your mind. It'll be dark red and probably weird in there. Wait a while for some thoughts. But don't get too distracted by them. You'll see that they just appear from nowhere. Like fish jumping out of water. It's like, la, la, la, nice ocean, few waves, hey, look at those clouds, BAM – fish leaps up and then splashes back down.

Dr Vladovski said consciousness is like watching a good film, being totally involved in it – feeling scared at the scary bits, happy at the happy bits, sad at the sad bits. But when you look really closely, you realise you're actually just watching coloured light on a screen . . .

Sorry, we got distracted again. I should stick to the story.

Where was I?

Oh yeah, that was *exactly* the problem – WHERE WAS I?!

At first I was confused when I couldn't see my body in the back of that minibus. By this time, Brian, Amy and Silent Cameraman had arrived in the zoo car park and were standing by my side. I was still in the body of Tito. I think this made it worse because male silverback gorillas can be pretty angry creatures. In the wild they fight each other and they go absolutely bananas (ha, bananas – perfect) when someone gets in their territory, or steals eggs from their nest. Also, when people film nature documentaries, presenters try not to make eye contact with alpha-male gorillas – apparently even that can wind them up. Window to the soul, remember?

So with all that in mind, I felt especially upset about the situation. In fact, it's safe to say, I overreacted. I leapt on to the bonnet of the minibus, feeling Tito's heavy body slam into the metal. The suspension groaned under my weight. Then I punched a hole in the windscreen – my strong black arm looked like a hairy tree trunk. I grabbed the whole pane of glass and ripped it out, flinging it over my shoulder.

'Hey!' someone said. 'Chill out!'

I turned to look and heard a deep, terrifying roar – it came from my mouth – then I whacked myself on the chest a few times. Maybe chilling out was good advice?

Nah.

Instead, I jumped high, landing on the roof of the minibus. The metal panels warped and dented as I swung both fists down into it again and again and – why not? – again.

The rest happened in a bit of a blur. I had just pulled one of the wheels off and bounced it across the car park with a grunting huff when I saw a tiny pale hand on my arm.

'Chester.' It was a girl. It was Amy. Just Amy. 'Calm down,' she whispered. 'Calm down.'

All right, yes, I thought, sitting on the ground. To my left, the minibus was destroyed – every window shattered, the driver's seat snapped in half, all the cushion foam spread across the tarmac. I'd even yanked out bits of the engine. Brian was holding his shoulder and wincing in pain. I must have knocked him over or something. Silent Cameraman was standing next to his camera, which had been smashed on the floor. I guess Tito didn't like being filmed.

Just like when I was a squirrel and I wanted to climb trees and bury nuts, now, trapped in Tito, I had a short temper and a strong urge to find fruit (gorillas eat mostly fruit – that fact is definitely true). Also, I wanted to search through Amy's hair and nibble her fleas.

She stroked my shoulder.

'Whurgh,' I said. 'Whurgh muh uuh-dy?'

She looked over at the minibus.

'Whurgh ah eh?'

I was trying to say, 'Where am I?' But gorillas don't have quite the same vocal chords as humans.

'We don't know, Chester.' Just Amy seemed to understand. 'The police are on their way.'

The officer who arrived had never seen or even heard of the show, so explaining the problem proved tricky.

'Sorry, start again,' he said, with his notepad ready.

'Someone has kidnapped my brother,' Amy explained.

'But . . . but you said your brother is a gorilla?'

During this conversation, I was hiding behind the damaged minibus. Brian said it would be best. We'd basically stolen a gorilla from the zoo. They'd be wanting it back pretty soon.

'No,' Amy said. 'Chester's *consciousness* is in the

gorilla. His actual *body* is missing. Maybe you should look around for some evidence?'

'OK.' The police officer laughed. 'Hey, come on down to the station. I think I know who can help you.' He handed Amy a card and stepped towards his car. 'Ask for him at reception. Have a nice day.'

And, with a smile and a wave, the officer left. I had a feeling he didn't believe us.

Amy said it would be a shame not to film this trip to the police station, which made me frown and blow air out of my nostrils. This was a stressful time and I wasn't really in the mood for doing tricks on camera.

Brian patted my huge forearm and said, 'Chest-o, I know this must be really hard for you. If you want to stop the show just nod and we'll delay the second series. We can pick up once this is all sorted.'

However, Amy looked over to me and shook her head. Maybe she was right. This pickle would probably be resolved by the end of the day – maybe it was silly to give up.

It might affect our pay too.

'Whurgh-eh-urrgh,' I grumbled (trying to say 'whatever').

Red Rose Pictures sent another minibus, which Brian drove to the police station.

On the way, I sat in the back and tried to get my thoughts in line. What was I thinking? That someone was behind this. But who? Was it possible the—

'Steeerhg Gwemmers.'

'Pardon?' Amy leant close to listen.

'Deh – pepple.'

She closed her eyes. 'Say that again.'

'Bahd pepple. Cuhlt.'

'Nope. Didn't get a word of it.'

'Pehhn. Geh mah pehhn.' I pretended to write.

'A pen?'

'Geeah.' I nodded. 'Pappa. Peeehn ah pappa.'

Brian passed a biro and a sheet of paper into the back of the minibus. It was difficult to hold it properly, especially with corners and bumps in the road. In the end I just gripped it with my fist, poked my tongue out and scrawled a few messy words. When I'd finished, I handed it to Amy.

71

'D ... B?' she tried to read, squinting at the wonky letters. 'D ... R?'

'Derhcteey.'

'Der ...? Oh, Doctor. Doctor ... Doctor Vladovski ...'

'Mmm.' I gave her a thumbs up.

'Worm? Wormed?'

'Neergh.'

'Worked? Wa ... *Warned*.'

'Eh, eh, geah.'

'About the store ... the store in ... Swindon?'

I covered my face and groaned.

'As in the town?'

'Urrrrrgh.'

'Sorry, Chester, it's just ... OK. St ... Star? Yes? Star ... Swim ... star swimmers? Dr Vladovski warned about the star swimmers. The ancient or ... order of ... of mind jumpers?'

Finally.

Dr Vladovski had told me that all this was dangerous. I hadn't seen him for months, since we started the show, so I was guessing he wouldn't be happy that I'd made mind jumping world-famous. But the star swimmers – who I was now sure existed – would be even less happy.

Maybe they've stolen my body as a punishment, I thought. Hey, maybe they've already lobbed it in the sea, or dropped it into a wood chipper? I felt a wave of terrible gorilla anxiety. Must avoid these negative thoughts. Dipped it in a piranha tank? No, stop.

We arrived at the police station and all walked across the car park. Amy, a seventeen-year-old girl in a white summery dress, scarf and denim jacket, Brian, in a smart shirt and grey trousers, Silent Cameraman in a black jumper, and me, in a twenty-five-stone silverback gorilla. It was at that moment I realised I was naked. Usually it didn't bother me when I was an animal – all animals are naked after all – but this was the longest I had ever been something other than myself. I felt oddly self-conscious as we entered the building. As soon as we got inside, I grabbed two magazines from the waiting-room table and used them to cover up. I held one at my front and one at my back.

Amy dinged the bell on the reception desk. A woman appeared.

'Good evening, what can I do for— AARRRGHH!'
she screamed. 'You can't bring a gorilla in here.'

'Well, with all due respect,' Amy said, 'clearly we
can. Look. There he is.'

The woman seemed alarmed. However, once she
saw that I was standing peacefully in my makeshift
magazine skirt, she calmed down.

'We need to speak to Detective Pepper,' Amy said,
presenting the card.

The receptionist eventually agreed to let us
through – which was actually pretty unprofessional
of her if you think about it.

'Thaungghhhks,' I grunted, giving her a nod.

She was white with fear. Was I *really* that frightening?
Oh, it was too tempting. After she opened the door
for us, she stepped quickly behind her desk and, as I
waddled past, I turned to her and smiled. Then, when
she half-smiled back, I *tried* to say 'boo'. But I misjudged
it, so I just roared, 'BAAAAAAAAAUUURGH!!' in
her face. It was loud enough for her to scream, fall
backwards over her swivel chair and then faint. Even
Brian and Amy leapt away in shock.

'So-reugh,' I said.

We arrived at Detective Pepper's office. Amy knocked and a voice said, 'Yeah, and wot?'

Inside, we saw a middle-aged man with black hair and a bit of a beer belly reading a newspaper. He was wearing a bright yellow Hawaiian shirt covered in pineapples, and a thick leather jacket. He also had one of those leather gun-holster strappy things – you know the kind that go over your shoulders. This was weird, because police in England don't even have guns.

'Evenin',' Detective Pepper said in a strange voice. I think it was like an East London accent, sort of cockney maybe? I don't know, but it sounded like he was trying to sound cooler than he actually was. 'And what can I do for you lot?' He looked over his newspaper at me, frowned, then nodded. 'Dat, dat right there – dat is one of the best costumes I've ever seen. If not *the* best. I fink the eyes, the mask, that's what sells it.'

Brian and Silent Cameraman also entered.

Detective Pepper lifted an eyebrow – he seemed to change when he spotted the camera. His belly shrunk and his chest puffed out as he sucked himself in to look better. 'What's all this then, eh? Filming somethin'?'

'We were wondering if you'd be able to help us,' Amy said. 'Someone has kidnapped my brother.'

I handed him the note I'd written in the minibus.

'Even them fingers look real,' he said, taking the piece of paper. He turned back to Amy. 'How can you be so sure?'

'What?' she said.

'Kidnap means someone done it, yeah? How you know he ain't just 'opped a fence and legged it, eh?'

'Because he's ... His mind is here, in this gorilla – it's his *body* which is gone. And it would be in a sort of trance, so it wouldn't be able to run away.'

'Rehd gaah nohte,' I grunted, pointing.

'Hang about, this fancy-dress nonsense – this your brother? The one who's missin'? Nah, nah, nah,' Detective Pepper said, waving his hand. 'Not for me. I know a wind-up when I see it – you're havin' a giggle. Can't prank Pepper.'

'Just Google *Amy and Chester*,' she said, glancing at the camera and rolling her eyes.

Suddenly alert, Detective Pepper sat up, slamming

his newspaper on his desk. 'Oi oi, nah, nah, naaaaah, easy, you're Amy Parsons?'

'Yes.'

'So . . . monkey chops 'ere is the wheaty puff kid?'

I groaned.

'That's right.'

'I fought that show was all fake?' he said. 'Like, tricks and that?'

'Nope,' Amy said. 'All real.'

'Well fry my socks and sell me a pound-a-strawberries. Ya-know-what-I-mean?'

'Not really.'

'Sounds like trouble. I'm not interested in the case. You'll have to find someone else.'

I was frowning a lot now – why was no one taking this seriously?

'Oh my, that's a terrible shame,' Brian said. 'You'd have been a real hit on the show.'

Again, this caught his attention. 'Wait, wait, wait, I'd be on the show? Me? Like, proper like?'

'Well, of course,' Brian said. 'And you'll be a hero if you find him.'

Out of everyone, Brian seemed the most concerned about my well-being. At first I thought he was being kind – but then I realised it was also a matter of money. He *needed* me to be OK. I was, after all, the star of the show. If anything happened to Chester Parsons, his career was over. He wanted to find me, and soon. This was comforting. I knew he would do anything to get me back safely.

'Please,' Brian whispered. 'You *have* to find him.'

'Awwww, maybe I was being too hasty. Bit tired. I was on the sauce last night drinkin' moon juice with ol' Stanley Baxter from the docks.' This was something Detective Pepper did a lot – I think, like me, his mind wandered. Except he said it all out loud. 'He's a good boy. Gave me this shirt. Ya like it?'

I grunted. Impatient gorillas get things moving.

Finally, he read my note.

'Ancient order of mind jumpers?' Detective Pepper said. 'What do we know about 'em? Shady organisation I bet. How's this for a plan, eh? We get in the motor, we cruise over to Dr Vladovski's place, grab him by his collar, say, "Oi, Vladovski, tell us what you know. Tell us right naaah." Maybe we go to the drive-through. Maybe we buy some vanilla milkshakes. Who's with me?'

We arrived at forty-three Sandy Street half an hour later. Silent Cameraman got some shots of the building, then we all entered together. On the way we had stopped off and bought me a pair of XXXL shorts, on account of my nudity, so I could finally ditch the magazines.

When we came into the reception area, Detective Pepper stepped forwards first. 'Right, listen here, love,' he said to the receptionist, slamming his milkshake on the desk. 'Dr Vladovski, where is he?'

She frowned. 'Dr Vladovski?'

'Yeah, Niko Vladovski. Russian. Bear-charmer. Therapist. Mad geezer. Bald. Beard. Come on. Don't give us ya frowny face – *where is he*?'

'Dr Vladovski used to work here,' she whispered. 'But he died almost thirty years ago ...'

I let out a deep gasp of shock. What the hell was going on? Had I been hypnotised by a ghost? What was happening, what the—

'Only joking,' she said. 'But he did leave. I just came in one day and his office was empty. Everything gone.'

'Any idea where he went?' Amy asked.

'He didn't say. It was as though he had some very important business to attend to ... Sorry, is that a gorilla?' No one answered.

'So guys,' Loser Amy said into the camera. 'Just to bring you up to speed, it seems like—'

Detective Pepper barged in front of her. 'Right, listen to this,' he said, pointing at the camera, leaning into it. 'Bloke's got a wonky name, hook for a hand. Chester says he's a diamond but nah, nah, nah. Sounds more like a prime suspect if you ask me. Pull ya socks up, sailors – this case is about to get *naughty*.'

And then, without another word, he kicked the door open and strutted out of the room.

'Quite strange, isn't he?' Amy said. We all nodded.

Chapter 6

The Bloodstained Journal

We had a break from filming so Amy and I were able to go home. It was here we came across the first major clue of the investigation. First Major Clue Alarm – *ding, ding, ding*. Wait. No. No alarms for clues – that kills the suspense. Damn. Forget about the clue. Just . . . la, la, la – hey, remember when I was auditioning to be a potato? Great day.

Anyway.

So there I was, or rather, there I *wasn't*, up in Amy's bedroom. She put a towel down on her bed and I perched on the mattress, the springs groaning under my weight.

'Just, don't . . . don't touch anything,' she said.

It had been a fair while since I lost my body and I was *still* trying to mind jump out of this gorilla. I could control the anger, but the urge to eat everything and leap about the place, maybe flip over the odd table and beat my chest and throw poo, was becoming hard to resist. Vladovski was right. Being out of yourself too long wasn't good for you. Felt like I was getting ill. Like maybe I hadn't eaten enough or couldn't breathe properly or something. It's quite hard to explain.

Not sure how I felt about Dr Vladovski. He seemed so cool. He taught me some great stuff – but why would he leave without telling anyone? What important business did he have? What if . . . what if he wasn't who he said he was? Maybe *he* was part of this ancient order? Maybe that's why he warned me – he wanted to keep it a secret?

I couldn't be sure. We left a message on his mobile explaining that my body was missing and that he really should return the call. But no response.

Instead of worrying, I decided to focus all my efforts on escaping this hairy primate prison. Just Amy was sitting opposite me, at the other end of the bed with her laptop. She was googling Dr Vladovski over and over again, but I was staring deep, deep into her eyes.

Come on, you can do it. Just jump. Dive. Swim into Amy's brain. Come on. Come on …

'Hey, Chester, you should read this – it says—'

Zip-whoosh.

I flinched and looked down at myself. Yes. Excellent. YES. I was in Amy's mind.

'It worked,' I said, in her voice. 'Oh, that feels better.'

Unlike last time, she realised straight away what I'd done.

'Chester,' she shouted. 'Chester, get out.'

Amy leapt to her feet and stomped to her mirror. I could see that she was annoyed – she had previously banned me from ever going in her head, which I suppose is fair enough. But this *was* an emergency. She stared directly into her own eyes.

'Seriously, I told you *never* to do this again.'

'Amy, relax,' I (she) said. 'This is good news. I can actually still do it.'

If anyone had seen us, it would have looked like she

was simply standing in front of her mirror having an argument with herself.

'I don't care. I don't want you in here. Plus, look.' We turned to Tito. 'That's just a silverback gorilla now. What's he going to do?'

'Yeah, that's a fair point.'

However, Tito seemed relaxed on the bed, pouting and frowning, scratching his stomach.

'He is big, isn't he?'

Tito sniffed and took deep breaths, his huge chest bulging. Then he tapped Amy's bamboo wind chimes dangling near the window. The noise seemed to upset him. Grunting, he yanked them – the string snapped and then, as though he was curious, he started biting the wood.

'Hey!'

Tito glanced at Amy and sighed, throwing the broken wind chimes over his shoulder.

'Chester – this is dangerous.'

I turned Amy back to the mirror. 'Listen, maybe this means something. Maybe my body is ... I dunno ... asleep somewhere? Maybe the people who moved it unsettled me? But now it's relaxed again? That's why I've got the ability back?'

'Fine, good, you can mind jump again. Now get back in your gorilla.'

'Your brain is so weird,' I said, thinking. 'Everything is so ... Yeah ... You see the world in a strange way.'

'Stop it.'

'So many unusual thoughts in here. Ooh, memories ... Any good secrets I wonder?'

Amy rolled her eyes back, as though she could somehow find me that way. 'Seriously, no.' She hit the side of her head. It hurt us both, but I carried on. I knew this wasn't a nice thing to do but that little voice had returned – go on, why not, it'll be funny. Besides, sometimes she was mean to me ...

And then I found something important, something crucial.

'Whoa ... the stickman with three eyes,' I said. 'You've seen that symbol before? You can remember it. Wait. Wait. Where? Think, Amy, think *where* have you seen that image?'

'I can't remember – I can't think clearly with you in here.'

'Hang on ... I'm feeling ... What is this? Shame,' I said. 'There *are* secrets in here ... Don't think about ... don't think about ...'

I browsed through Amy's memories. Some of it was gross – like how she felt about this guy at college. It seemed as though the things she was trying *not* to think about were the very thoughts that kept leaping into her mind.

'Who's Zack?' I said in a funny voice. As it was coming out of Amy's mouth it sounded especially high-pitched. 'Zack. Zack ... What a terrible name. Aw ... this is *horrible*. I think you're the one who needs therapy, Amy. And now you're talking to yourself as well?'

'Chester, please, stop looking in there.'

'Something ... something you're trying not to think ... something about ... a lock? Or ... or a gate? Gate. Gate? Is there—'

'No.' She scrunched up her face and squeezed her head. But it was too late. I had seen it.

'Amy...it was you?' I said. '*You* left the side gate open?'

'Chester, I'm sorry.'

'Dandelion is dead because of YOU?' I yelled. 'You had me believing it was my fault. You've probably done me actual psychological harm. Gah. All this time. This is ... You ... Right ... I'm going to mess you up.'

I was furious, even without those gorilla hormones. For years, *years*, I had blamed myself. I looked into the mirror again – into my sister's evil eyes. She was pulling a doubly angry face – she was angry that I was in her mind, *I* was angry that she was a liar, a dog-killing psycho. I wanted to cut her hair, or burn all her things or ... or ...

I bit her arm.

'Ouch, damn,' I said.

This was another thing I had discovered about myself – sometimes, when I get upset, especially with Amy, I feel like doing really crazy stuff. Once I smashed her favourite mug after she flicked me with an elastic band. Usually I can stop and calm down. But this time, it was like I had no control – like a bad part of my personality had taken over.

'Where's your phone?'

'No.'

'You've left me no choice,' I yelled, as I grabbed her bag and started rifling through it.

Amy's right hand seemed to be under her command and was tugging at her left hand, which I was using to pull lipstick and headphones and other random junk from her stupid smelly bag.

'Stop. No.'

'Yes. Yes, Amy. It's happening.'

I found her phone, pulled it out, then she threw herself on the floor. But I rolled her over, pinning her right arm down. Her legs were kicking and struggling.

'Get out of my mind!'

'I'm sorry, Amy, but you brought this on yourself.'

Scrolling through her contacts list, I noticed that Tito was watching us from the bed. Even a gorilla could see that this was a weird scene. A teenage girl rolling around on the carpet, fighting with herself.

At the bottom of the list, I found what I was after. Zack. Oh, handsome Zack. I pressed the little green icon.

'Chester, no.'

'Be quiet, Amy. This is an important call.'

I put the phone on loudspeaker and slid it away from us. It rang twice and then he answered.

'Zack,' I groaned, wrestling with Amy's body – she was arching and shaking like a panicked dolphin on a boat. 'No! Don't listen . . . Listen . . . I just want to say that I lo— NO.' She slammed a hand over her mouth, I tugged it away. 'Grrrahhh. Yes. I wanted to tell you that I love you and want— Stop. Zack, hang up, it's me, Amy, just hang up the— PLEASE listen to me, Zack. This is important. I want to marry you and have your— BASICALLY, Zack, I've been dared to ring you and— UUURGH, NO. NO.'

Amy regained control, scrabbled along the floor and dived for her phone. She grabbed it, but I snatched it from her with her left hand and it went spinning across the room. We turned and saw that Tito had caught the mobile. He sniffed it, then held it to his ear.

'Amy, what's going on?' Zack's voice asked.

Tito frowned, looked at the phone, and snapped it in half.

'Tito, no!' Amy yelled.

'Good boy, Tito.'

The gorilla roared, jumped off the bed and hit his chest. He seemed suddenly angry. Then, with bold dark eyes, he started marching forwards, his huge black arms swaying in rage. 'Uh-oh.'

'Chester, Chester, Chester.'

A blink and a deep gasp and I could see Amy on the floor, holding her hands up. Back in the gorilla, I turned around and sat on the carpet in the corner. I was sad now. I felt sorry for Amy. When I was in her mind, I felt just how guilty she was about the whole gate thing. She cried too when Dandelion died. Also, I could feel how badly she wanted people to like her, particularly Zack. I had definitely done some damage.

Maybe I had gone too far. Nah. Yes. Yes. It was mean. Amy didn't deserve that. Or maybe she did. No.

'Sorraarggh,' I said.

She stood, sniffed and picked up what was left of her mobile. 'I wanted to tell you, Chester. I walked around town all night looking for her.'

I knew that was true.

Nodding, I got us back on track. I grabbed a pen

and paper from her desk, and drew the three-eyed stickman. Then I pointed at it and grunted.

'I . . . I have no idea,' she said. 'Maybe you mentioned it and I imagined it?'

'Nuh.'

It was *definitely* a memory. An old one too. Amy *had* seen that picture. But where? The image in her mind was gloomy.

'Somehhaaar aaark?' I wrote on the notepad. 'Somewhere dark?'

'Somewhere dark . . .' She closed her eyes. 'Yeah . . . I have seen it . . . in . . . in . . . Wait . . .'

Amy strode out of her room and into the hall. I followed her past the porthole window (we used to pretend the hallway was a submarine when we were younger – I miss those games). She pulled on the cord for the attic ladder, which came swinging down with a dusty thud.

She climbed up quickly, lifting herself through the hatch and into the shadow of the loft. I followed, but my wide shoulders got stuck in the opening. With a wriggle I managed to get both elbows on the floorboards, still standing on the ladder, my head poking up and glancing around. She slid a large box forward. It was marked 'Dad's stuff'.

You may have noticed I haven't mentioned my dad so far. Well that's because he died when I was a baby, so I have no memories of him. I basically never think about the guy. Amy and Mum said he was brilliant though.

There were a few random folders and odd pieces of junk, but then she pulled out a leather-bound book. An old journal of some kind. It was entitled *An Ancient Evil*. She threw it over to me. I read the cover. 'The tale of the thousand-year-old body thief. By W.E.'

Then Amy lifted a small statue, a metal man with three eyes instead of two.

'Oooorrrghh,' I said.

She passed it to me. I inspected the figure – my black finger and thumb were ridiculously big next to the tiny model.

Placing the little man on the wooden floor of the loft, I turned my attention back to the book. On the spine, I noticed there was a red mark – it looked like dried blood. Holding it to my nose, I sniffed.

Then I opened the journal carefully – it felt fragile. Inside, all the pages were gone. They had been torn from the spine. Weird. However, something fell out. Old brown paper, stained and crinkled like a treasure map, landing in front of me like a clue I was meant to find. It was a note. A handwritten message.

Jack, (That was my dad's name.)

The Whispered Truth are the star swimmers. The name is just a front. The Whispered Manor is where they sleep. They have answers to questions you should never ask. You kick hornet nest, you get stung. My advice is to run.

Your friend,
Niko Vladovski

'Braaeergghffguurrrg!' I yelled, holding the note up for Amy. She took it from me and frowned as she read.

'Dad knew Dr Vladovski?' she said. 'That doesn't make sense ... and the star swimmers? Chester, we should ... we should ... we should be filming all this.'

Chapter 7

The Rat Trap

The plan was simple: we needed to go to a place called the Whispered Manor. That, according to the note in the attic, was where the star swimmers were based.

But we couldn't do it alone. And besides, as Amy said, we were meant to be filming everything for the show.

So we contacted Detective Pepper, who arrived at our house with Brian and Silent Cameraman. We had already asked Mum about the note and she was just as confused as we were. However, Brian said we had to ask her again, but on camera. This was a ridiculous thing they made us do every now and then. Brian said even the most authentic reality shows have to 'bend the definition sometimes'.

We were filming in the dining room.

'Hey guys,' Amy said into the camera, with dramatic hands. 'So just to bring you up to speed with the investigation. Doctor Vladovski has totally gone missing – I know, right? Crazy. But get this, Chester and I found a book in our loft with a note from Vladovski to *our dad*.' She held up the piece of paper, presenting it like a product she was trying to sell. 'As if that's not confusing enough, our dad died over ten years ago.'

'Yah, OK. Hang on, Amy,' Brian said. 'Say that bit again, but slower – bit more intense. Let's get the mystery vibe right at the front.'

I sighed.

'Go from, "But get this . . ."'

Amy was happy to jump through these hoops.

'But get this,' she said, 'we found a book in our loft with a note from Vladovski to our dad . . . And as if that's not crazy enough . . . our dad died over ten years ago . . .'

'Yah, fab, fab,' Brian said. 'Now, we need some shots of you looking at the statue and the book on the table. Oh, yah, maybe some shots of your loft if poss?'

All this faffing around was annoying. I still didn't

know how long you could be outside of your body without damaging yourself. And I *still* couldn't help thinking about all the awful things that might have happened to it. Maybe it had been left out in the cold? Or in the sun? Maybe it'd been thrown off a roof? Stuffed and mounted on a wall – a Chester trophy? Why would someone do that?

No. Stop. Focus on solutions. Stick to the plan.

Either way, we needed to be *quick*. That seemed obvious. Surely the priority was my body – not making sure we'd got the best shots for the show? That's why, after watching Detective Pepper adjust his hair in the mirror for the fiftieth time, I stood, slammed my fists on the dining table and yelled, 'Huhhrrrry uuurrrgghppp.'

Which was, if you don't speak gorilla, 'Hurry up'.

I looked down and noticed the table was completely smashed – pieces of wood and splinters around my feet. I was strong.

'Riiiight, maybe,' Brian said with shocked eyes, '*maybe* we should take a more passive approach to filming from now on?'

'Yearrgh.' I nodded. 'Maaaybeeh. Yearrgh, goohh ideaah.'

'Fly on the wall kind of thing?'

'Fine by me, chief,' Detective Pepper said.

'So I'll just roll myself back, yah,' Brian whispered. 'No more interfering until this is resolved. Film what you can,' he said to Silent Cameraman, 'but priority is obviously finding Chest-o's bod. I'll head back to the studio and calm them down. Boss is panicked about all this. Darlings, I fear if this isn't over soon my career will be . . .' Brian looked as though he was going to cry. 'We should have guarded the minibus. Chest-o, I'm so sorry.'

I groaned and waved my hand. This wasn't anyone's fault. Well, apart from the star swimmers. I knew nothing about them besides the fact they are 'more dangerous than most angry bear you ever see' and they happily steal children's bodies. At least, that was my theory and the note we'd found made it seem all the more likely.

'Don't you worry about ya job, sunshine,' Detective Pepper said, patting Brian on the back. 'I solve cases like this for breakfast.'

Before he left, Brian gave me a gadget – it was like a small tablet with a screen about double the size of my phone.

'This is a speech generator,' he said. 'Meant for people with disabilities. See, you can type responses, it has predictive text, set phrases, yah, yah? Should help you a bit.'

I typed, 'Hey, this is pretty handy,' and the machine read it out. Then I tapped the 'ha' button as fast as I could. 'Ha. Ha. Ha. Ha. Ha. Ha.'

The electronic voice wasn't perfect. But my choices were limited. I could either speak like a robot, or like a gorilla.

'Thank you, Brian,' it said. I grunted in satisfaction. It was quite easy to use too. Even with these massive thumbs I was still pretty fast at typing.

From that moment on, Silent Cameraman simply filmed us. For the first time, the show was actually a *reality* show. Which is to say, we were acting as ourselves. Well, apart from Loser Amy's commentary. And, as you have probably noticed, Detective Pepper was basically insane, so it was hard to know when he was being himself and when he was acting up for the camera.

The Whispered Manor was about two hours from home. We all stepped out on to the driveway and round to Detective Pepper's old car. It looked like one of those soft-top American muscle cars you see in movies from the 1970s. Nice leather seats too.

'Maybe you should drive, Amy?' he said. 'I could run through the case on the way?'

'Nuuurgh.' I scrabbled with my voice tablet, trying to type no.

'No probs,' she said.

Silent Cameraman got in the back with me. I noticed that Detective Pepper's car had been fitted with two cameras in the front and a small one on the bonnet.

'Did some digging on 'em, didn't I,' he said, holding up a folder. 'These whispered geezers are lunatics. It's a cult of some kind, yeah. They shuffle about the place wearing robes. Meditating and that.'

'This is a nice car,' Amy said, stroking the steering wheel.

'Oh, she is a beauty,' Detective Pepper agreed. 'I got this motor from a fella used to work down the market – he sold flowers, biggest bunches you ever seen. Tulips. Orchids. Best prices in London.'

Amy pulled away and the car rumbled down the drive.

'Guy had some trouble,' he told us, speaking ridiculously fast as he sometimes did. 'Market got robbed. He needs someone to recover his flowers dun he? He's on the blower, ring ring. Hello. It's Pepper. Hour later I've got the toerags in cuffs. Gave me this as payment.' Detective Pepper patted the dashboard. 'I say no, that's too much – he says I'm his hero. He says if I was a woman he'd marry me. I said the car will be enough thanks very much goodnight.'

The wheels jolted as Amy got the hang of the brakes.

'Cor she's keen on the old pedals this one. Point is, motor's rough about the edges but she's got sentimental value. Been on some journeys, I tell ya. Monkey chops probably gets it. I bet there's a part of you that loves that gorilla?'

I was certainly grateful to have Tito. Better to have a body than not.

The building was like a broken castle. Every section of its roof was a spike – as if dark rocks had been dragged into the sky like iron filings reaching for a magnet (magnets are cool aren't they?). A huge wall around the grounds was covered with ivy and CCTV cameras posted on all the corners searched for possible intruders. Above, wispy clouds seemed purple and grey – as though the place had its own climate.

'The Whispered Truth?' Detective Pepper said, peering out of the passenger window of his car, curling his top lip and frowning. 'Who'd call their cult that eh?'

'Suppose it makes sense they'd have a nickname,' Amy whispered. 'The star swimmers want to stay under the radar.'

We'd parked opposite the entrance – a tall steel gate opened up to the rest of the manor. It looked like there was the main structure, then lots of other newer buildings around it. If it wasn't for all the security, it could be mistaken for an old boarding school. I saw a few pigeons on the perimeter wall. They seemed to be staring right at us.

Was my body in there? Hidden in the Whispered Manor? I felt it might be.

'I didn't even know places like that existed in this country,' Amy said.

'Plenty of old gaffs about,' Pepper added. 'Went on a ghost hunt once in Scotland. Spooky abandoned church. Saw a little girl in a white dress with the face of a horse. She was laughing and running around. Real creepy ya know. I was like, *what* is this nonsense? Didn't sleep for a week. Found out later it was just a mask. Good job I didn't kick her, cos I tell ya, I was tempted.'

'O ... K?'

There was also a person at the front gate – he was in one of those little outbuildings like a car-park attendant at an airport. A completely bald kid, about my age, wearing a long white robe. When he spotted us, he walked calmly out into the road and stood by the passenger door.

'Oi oi, look lively. Not ya typical security guard.' Detective Pepper wound down the window.

'May I help you?' the strange robed boy asked. He spoke with a soft, gentle voice and kept his hands clasped together at his stomach.

Although I wanted to grab him and give him a rough gorilla interrogation, I thought it best to let Detective Pepper do the talking.

'We're just having a little goosey, ya know.'

'You cannot film here, sir.'

'Nice dress, matey pops.'

'It is not a dress. Please leave or I will be forced to call the police.'

'You'd dial up the old bill 'cos of some friendly bants?' Detective Pepper turned to the camera and tutted. 'Listen to this doughnut.'

'Final warning, sir.'

'Hang about, buckle up ya boots, kids, we got ourselves a feisty one. What's your name, lad?'

'A whispering brother holds attachments not to this world.'

'You wot, mate?'

'We do not have names. Part of the initiation ritual is to let go of— My goodness, is that a gorilla?'

'Yeah, it's a gorilla, and wot? Scared of a gorilla?'

'Well, yes, of course.'

'Now why not open this gate – we wanna have a little chinwag with ya boss.'

'Cold Rain does not meet with outsiders.'

'Cold Rain?' Amy said. 'Thought you didn't have names?'

'Elders do. If you are not in possession of a search warrant, you have no business being here. Especially not with wild animals.'

'All right.' Detective Pepper pointed at him. 'But you put the kettle on cos we're coming back, you understand? Let's do one.' He patted his dashboard.

There was an awkward silence.

'Amy, I said, let's do one. Which means go.'

'Oh, sorry.' She fumbled with the gearstick.

'That was the coolest thing of the whole conversation and you mucked it up.' Detective Pepper looked at Silent Cameraman. 'I'll say it again.' But the robed guy was already leaving. 'Oi, come back. Oi, mate.

Put the kettle on. Let's roll.' Amy pulled away. 'Milk one sugar,' Detective Pepper yelled out of the window. 'Milk one sugar, ya sausage.'

The car stalled. The robed kid just stared as we pulled away again.

'Aw, you've proper ruined this one, Amy.'

We drove around the corner and parked up a little way down the street. The huge perimeter wall was still in sight. It looked like we were the other side of the castle grounds now, near a concrete area with a load of wheelie bins. I spotted two brown rats sniffing around the rubbish.

'So,' I typed. 'Does that mean we have to wait for a seated warfare?' I groaned. Stupid predictive text. 'Search warrant.'

'Where on earth am I gonna get a search warrant from eh?' Detective Pepper said.

'Um, I dunno, through a judge?' Amy said. 'Or however it's done? You're the police officer.'

'Eh? Wot? I ain't no police officer.'

'Wheearrgh?!' I yelled.

'Nah, nah, nah, I'm a private investigator innit.'

'Why the hell do you have an office at the police station then?' Amy asked.

'Sometimes the cops get a case that's too hot for 'em, ya know? They dial my number. Ring, ring. Hello, it's Detective Pepper, I'm in my dressing gown, dinner's on, I'm having shepherd's pie with raspberry sauce, make it fast, what do ya need? We've got a case, they say, it's dangerous, ya know. It's risky, it's high stakes. We need the Big Shaker. We need the best damn detective in the country. And I say, well, lucky for you, I happen to know who that is. Here's ya first clue. It's me.'

'All right, guys,' Amy said to the camera. 'Another interesting revelation, seems we've crossed some wires here. But luckily we've hired the best damn detective in the country to solve the case. So that's good. Oh, news just in.' Amy put her finger to her ear. 'Looks like the sarcasm-o-metre just exploded.'

'Hahhg,' I laughed. That was Just Amy. See, she's sometimes funny.

'Easy tiger,' Detective Pepper said. 'We're not in the playground. Even if I could get a search warrant I wouldn't play by the book. That ain't me.'

'So what do you suggest?' I said. Yes, no typos!

'I suggest we drive right through that front gate, grab this Cold Rain bloke, slam him into the dirt and say, oi rainy chops, spill ya wisdom, ya dirty scamp. Tell us where Chester's body is. And if he refuses we give him a little slap. If he still refuses . . . well . . . we give him another slap.'

'Sure . . . that sounds good,' Amy said. 'Or maybe we wait till dark and let Chester sneak in there and look for his body.'

'Aw yeah, great idea,' Detective Pepper said. 'Send the silverback on the sneaking mission. Makes sense, well done, Amy. Run that through ya sarcasm-o-metre eh. What's my score?'

'Six. But I never said Chester should take Tito with him,' Amy whispered, pointing at the rats near the bin.

We strapped Tito in place with seat belts and snacks, then I jumped across the road into my new body. It was such a relief to have the ability back – it made me feel powerful, made me feel *free*. Small, brown fur, odd smell. Yep. Done. I was in control of this creature. The mind of a rat is not usually very interesting. But *this rat* was different.

I found a tight hole in the wall, crawled in and scurried through the cold grass towards the main castle. It was dark and the stars above seemed daunting now I was so close to the ground. My path into the building was obvious – I could smell the way to the kitchen. I could smell the cool mud beneath me. I could smell the bin juice on my scraggy fur.

Near some weeds, a little way from the back door, I found a vent panel. Two slats at the bottom were broken – looked like they'd been chewed through. I ran up and into the vent shaft.

My claws tapped on the shiny metal as I scurried along, stopping from time to time to smell the air with my fast twitching nose. A little *sniff-sniff-sniff*.

At the end of the narrow tunnel I stopped. I could smell something new.

Cheese.

Yum.

I turned a corner. And there it was, right in the middle of the tunnel. Waiting for me. Lit by a heavenly beam of orange light from the vent slats by its side. Like, *aaaaaah*, choir-singing. Without thinking, I scampered along towards the food. Wait. Stop, I thought. No. *But, yes.* No. *But cheese?* I was standing right in front of the small, delicious cube of cheddar now. Beautiful and yellow, rich and heavy. A perfect little lump of dairy gold. Aw man, it looked fresh too – a slight shine and mark down the side from a knife.

Sniff-sniff-sniff. Whiskers tickling the sides of the vent shaft.

I wanna eat that cheese so bad. Imma do it. No, stop. It's a mousetrap, look. See the spring? That piece of metal will swing down and smash your skull. *Sure, but cheese. Free cheese.* Well, it's not free, is it. It'll cost your life. *I don't understand.* (I had found a really clever, argumentative rat. Why was its consciousness so switched on?) Why are you so smart? I thought. Huh?

What do you mean?

Well, I'm thinking, I thought, but I can hear you thinking too?

I'm confused.

So, right, you know you have an internal monologue, like a voice in your head?

Sure.

Well, why have you got one, if you're a rat? And why are you arguing with me?

Sorry, I think we've got off on the wrong paw – who are you?

I'm Chester Parsons.

Pleased to meet you.

Are you ... I mean, do you have a name?

A whispering brother holds attachments not to this world.

Wait ... what? You're one of them?

Of all the rats I could have picked, I had found one that was already occupied. Two mind jumpers. Two consciousnesses. Both competing for control of a single, greedy little rodent.

We eating this cheese or what?

If you're a human, how come you can't see that this is clearly a mousetrap?

Exactly. Mouse. We're a rat. It's not for us. It'll probably be fine. Let's eat it.

Please, no.

Look, Chester, you knew the risks. Now get ready because it's five past cheddar and I am hungry.

Before I could stop myself, I felt my tiny mouth open, jut forwards and clamp on the cube of cheese. I heard a click, then closed my eyes and waited for death.

Chapter 8

Peace, Calm and Gorilla Tranquillity

This terrible mousetrap cheese incident highlighted a very interesting question. What happens if the body you're in dies? Does your consciousness go somewhere else? Is there an afterlife? Short answer is . . . drum roll . . . no.

Sorry to be the one to break it to you, but this is it. Straight up. So take good care of your body. Definitely don't lose the thing. If there's a moral to this whole story, that would be it. Don't lose your body – it's the only one you're getting.

You're probably miffed about the afterlife thing.

Fine. There *might* be an afterlife. Happy now? The one thing I can tell you for certain is: if you're out mind jumping and you end up in a different body, and *that* body dies, you die with it. You don't go back to your first body. No retries. It's not like a saved game or anything. It's done. Over. Dead. Like, the stakes are as high as they seem.

Obviously this rat I was in wasn't *my* body, so I wasn't particularly attached to it. However, in the same way a car crash is so much worse if you're in the car, I did not want it to die.

But when I opened my eyes in that vent shaft, I was a) alive and b) eating some cheddar. Tasted expensive too.

See, told you, it's fine, the other consciousness in the rat thought. *Trap's a dud. I knew that all along.*

We stepped away with the cheese between our teeth and, a second later, with a terrifying bang, the trap snapped shut, bouncing, clattering, echoing around inside the vent shaft. We held the cheese in our small paws – our mouth hung open. The hard piece of springy metal had broken the wooden base. It would have easily decapitated a rat.

Or not, whatever. Just got to be quick. I felt my tiny shoulders lift with a shrug.

This was the weirdest conversation of my life – all done via thoughts in a rat brain. I wanted to know more about this guy. We stood in the dark vent shaft munching the cheese.

That was too close, I thought. Why aren't you more careful?

Huh?

You're a mind jumper right?

Um … yeah, maybe. Da … Daahsuti? That rings bells.

So you're a member of this cult, the Whispered Truth, a.k.a. the star swimmers?

Oh yeah, I think so.

You think so?

I … What was your name again?

Chester. How long have you been in this rat?

I dunno, maybe … a week? Cold Rain told me I had disobeyed the order. My punishment, demoted to rat.

That's quite mean.

Yeah. Sometimes other animals too. My friend's been a goldfish for years.

114

I'm not an expert on all this, I thought.

Clearly.

But you seem to have come to terms with it?

It's not the end of the world. Certainly less to worry about as a rat. Life is simple.

How long can you be out of your body?

It varies. But after a while you will forget stuff, like me. Soon enough you just dissolve, like a sugar cube in a glass of warm water. I have accepted things, although it does get lonely. Hey, maybe you could stay here and live with me? It's been great talking to you.

Nah, but thank you.

Suit yourself. What you even doing here anyway?

Right, yeah, maybe you can help me. I've lost my body.

Bummer.

Yes, bummer. I'm spending most of my time in a gorilla from the zoo.

Aw, cool. What's it like?

I dunno, horrible? It would be fun, but things are stressful at the moment.

You know, when I lost something, my mother used to say it was probably in the last place you left it.

I already checked there.

Hmmm, then I'm stumped.

I think the star swimmers stole it.

Who?

The ... the cult ... the Whispered Truth. The star swimmers. The people in this building.

Oh yeah. I'm one of them. Well, I used to be – did I mention I got exiled to rat?

Yes. Do you think it's possible they've stolen my body?

Why would they?

Well, because I've spoken publicly about mind jumping.

Oh, no, no, they don't like that.

I know.

As long as you didn't tell too many people, you should be fine.

I told EVERYONE. We made a TV show all about it.

Chester Parsons – I knew that name was familiar. Put a little smile on the Puff Puff Wheat P—

SHUT UP. All right, just shut up. Sorry, it's just ...
Of all the things you can remember.

It's a catchy jingle.

Look, if they have kidnapped me, where would my body be?

Well, it would be in the sleeping room with all the others.

Where's that?

Where's what?

The sleeping room.

Oh, in the basement. You tired?

Look, just take me there.

Aw, the cheese is all gone. I didn't even pay attention – completely missed it. You ever do that – your thoughts just wander?

All the time. Come on.

We scurried through the new vent shaft in the old building, stopping briefly at one open grill. Through the thin slats I could see a huge open hall below – it looked a bit like the inside of a church. There were thousands of candles, long red banner flags with the three-eyed stickman on some of the walls, golden ornaments and about a hundred bald people wearing white robes. They were all sitting cross-legged on the floor in total silence. I saw that most of them were children. The youngest were at the back. And they seemed to get older towards the front – like a school assembly, but the other way around. Some were about four or five years old, all the way up to grandad-aged people in the first row.

The room was foggy with smoke from loads of incense sticks jutting like strange burning plants out of pots of sand dotted around the place. Sitting on a step at the front of the room, near the altar I guess you could call it, was a man with dark hair tied in a long plait. Unlike the others, he was wearing a *black* robe. Everyone's eyes were closed. Looked like they were meditating.

What's going on down there? I thought. Is this . . . is this like a school for mind jumpers?

Kind of.

And him, at the front? Why isn't that guy bald like the others?

Oh, that's Cold Rain. He's in charge. Stay away from him. See that sword?

The man had a long object on his lap – like a katana, one of those cool Japanese swords.

Yeah, I thought.

Well, he isn't afraid to use it.

The only sound was the occasional cooing and shuffling of pigeons. I saw, at the back of the room, hundreds of wooden cages – a few grey feathers were on the stone floor, mixed with sawdust and ash.

What's with all the birds? I thought.

That's how the elders travel. If you get lost in a pigeon, at least it'll bring you home safely.

Elders? Who are they?

Star swimmers who can mind jump.

So not everyone here can do it?

What? No, of course not. It takes decades of practice to achieve your first real mind jump. Any longer than a few seconds is impossible without training. Some people never manage it.

I did it the first time I tried.

No, you didn't. The youngest ever Daahsuti master was twenty-three – it takes years. And once you manage it, it can still take days to recharge for your next one. See all those kids? They practise on pigeons, mice, cats – but none of them can do more than a minute without falling out or dissolving.

Well, I'm eleven and I've done it loads of times. All kinds of animals too. Even my sister.

Oh, now I know you're winding me up. I may be a rat but I'm not stupid. You're telling me you can mind jump people now?

Why, is that meant to be harder?

Ha, yeah. Simple minds are easy, but humans have the most complicated brains of all. Only a few have ever cracked it. And I'm talking grand masters – ancient practitioners who have spent hundreds and hundreds of years meditating.

I did it by accident. Actually, my first few jumps were on people.

I don't believe you. In fact, I don't even believe you're really a mind jumper at all.

Um, well, how do you think I got here?

Oh yeah, good point.

We came to the end of the shaft. There was a deep black shadow. We peered over the edge.

Right, it's straight down from here. Ready?

Carefully we stepped forwards. Our back legs held on for a second – I think the rat's instincts were kicking in. But they slipped and we fell, spinning in the dark, then thudded on to the metal of another floor.

Ouch.

Rats are pretty durable, don't worry.

Ahead, some light was coming through another opening. We arrived, stood on our hind legs and leant against the shaft's metal grill, wriggling and poking our head through. I saw another room, twice the size of the last one. It was gloomy in here and, on the floor, lined up in endless rows of wooden beds, people were sleeping. Children at one end, adults at the other.

What's this room all about?

When you're out practising, this is where your body sleeps. These are mostly elders. At the top are the masters. They're out doing the most important work.

The men at the far end were all very, very old. Long grey beards, those weird old-people spots on their bald heads and thin, frail bodies.

There were more pigeon cages down here too. One robed girl, about thirty years old, took a bird then sat on one of the empty beds. She held it in her lap, then lay flat. After a couple of seconds, she closed her eyes and the pigeon leapt down on to the ground, and hopped along the room all the way to an empty fireplace at the far end. Then it flapped and disappeared up the chimney. Instead of wood and flames, there were feathers and bird droppings in the black fireplace.

Off she goes. Hey, see that skinny guy, down there, just to the left of the stone pillar?

Yeah?

That was my body.

Was? What happens to it now?

It'll die soon and they'll bury it. Can't have long left.

(I definitely didn't want that to happen to me. Starving to death didn't seem ideal at all.)

Harsh. But wait, you don't seem that old? Maybe twelve?

Thirteen.

So how come you can mind jump then?

I can only do about twenty seconds out of my body. Didn't I explain? I've been exiled. It's a punishment. Cold Rain made me jump into a rat, then he put me in a

122

cell with no windows. So I was trapped. After an hour or so he let me out. But it was too late. I had lost the ability. Too much of me had dissolved into the rat's mind. Now it's just a matter of time.

That is really, really not OK.

Yeah, but what are you gonna do?

First, I'm going to find my body. Right, now where is it?

We squeezed through the vent grill and down into the sleeping room. As everyone was fast asleep, it wasn't hard to check them all. We scurried along the cold stone wall at the head of the beds, looking down at each person. At first I thought these were mostly boys, but there were plenty of bald girls too.

Not me, not me, not me, not me, not me, not me, not me, *not me*, I thought as we checked every last one. None of them are me?

Bummer.

Where else might I be?

Only other place would be upstairs in Cold Rain's quarters – in his personal cell.

Take me there.

Impossible. You need to open doors and stuff. You'd need better hands than these useless rat claws.

We looked down at our scruffy rodent form.

You'd need to blend in too – you have to go through the main hall to get to the stairwell. Rats aren't allowed in there.

Please do it for me? Just jump into your body and open the door. I'll scurry through.

I told you, I CAN'T mind jump any more. It's been way too long. But you're more than welcome to my body. Just bring it back in one piece – I want to be buried out in the orchard next to my grandfather.

That's kind, but also super weird, I thought. You sure it's cool?

It's a great idea – you'll look like everyone else. But don't let Cold Rain see you up close. He'll think it's me and I'm in massive, massive trouble.

What did you even do?

I tried to read Wise Earth's journal. I was curious about him – he's a legend. They say he went crazy, but I'm not so sure.

Wise Earth? What's with all these stupid names?

Wise Earth founded the star swimmers with Red Fire and Cold Rain. They'd be upset to hear you speaking ill of their names.

I don't care. Pack of losers.

Anyway, story goes that Wise Earth killed Red Fire a few years ago, then disappeared. That's why Cold Rain is in charge now. Apparently, things were much nicer around here under Wise Earth's command. They had some argument about how to run the star swimmers. But, as I say, he's long gone.

To be honest, I'm not really interested in the politics of all this. I just want my body back.

We scurried over to *his* body. His face was pale, his cheekbones sticking out below dark eye sockets. Although he looked sick, he seemed to be resting peacefully.

Right, Cold Rain's quarters are on the top floor. Follow the red banners to the stairwell. Then it's about twenty storeys up the tower and you can't miss it. I'll wait by the front door outside, near the steps. If anything goes wrong, just look out of the window and mind jump down to safety.

Thanks for the offer, but I'm not leaving here without myself. Hey, what was your name, before you joined these guys?

Um ... I can't ... It ... it was ... Carlos?

Well, Carlos, thank you for your help. If you ever need a place to stay, you can come be my pet rat.

Sorry, who are you again?

I took a small breath out, looked at Carlos's sleeping body and then, with that familiar whooshing sound, breathed in and opened my new eyes. I sat bolt upright in the bed and turned around. Behind me the small brown rat was trying to smile.

'No, Carlos,' I whispered. 'Rats can't really smile – that looks horrible.'

He squeaked. It must have been odd for him to see himself sit up and speak like this.

Having a human body felt amazing after all this time (it's just not the same in Amy's mind – there's too much conflict and being a teenage girl isn't really my thing). It's a bit like stretching your legs after a long car journey, or cracking your back after leaning over

126

for ages. It's like, *aaaaah* that's better. Still, as nice as Carlos's body was – it was a) really skinny and b) *not mine*. Staying in there long-term was not an option.

So I sneaked from the sleeping room, teasing open the huge oak door at the end of the hall. There was a narrow, spiral staircase made from stone. The steps were shiny in the middle, where they'd been walked on, and rough at the edges. I ran up quickly, holding my white robe around my knees like a skirt.

Down a corridor and I was in that main room, walking through the thick smoke, past all the pigeons in their cages. One cooed at me. Another flapped its wings a few times.

'Shh.'

To my left were the meditating kids, hundreds of them, all sitting cross-legged in total silence. It was weird seeing bald children. Right at the end was Cold Rain – he was the only one facing my way but, like the others, his eyes were closed.

I had to admit, the place was really peaceful and calm. Even the occasional noises from the pigeons didn't spoil it. I could have chilled out there all day.

But I had places to be. I reckoned that as long as I stayed quiet, as long as everything stayed this relaxed, I could creep through and get to the stairs easily.

So I tiptoed carefully round to the door, following the red banners on the wall just like Carlos had told me. I heard a few noises in the next room, which stirred a couple of the meditating children nearby – one turned and looked at me, but nodded then looked forwards again and disappeared into himself.

Once I felt it was clear, I gently pulled open the main door. Creaking, creaking, creaking on rusted hinges, like a treasure chest. And there, standing in front of me with thick, strong black arms, was a silverback gorilla.

I looked at Tito, Tito looked at me. Then I turned back to the room full of silent men, women and children.

'Tito,' I whispered. *'Be quiet.'*

Right, I would need to get back into him, I thought, before he kicked up a fuss. I stared, frowned, winced and knew almost instantly that I couldn't mind jump. Of course. Typical. It only worked *sometimes*. Hardly a superpower.

Luckily he seemed calm. Until, that is, one of the people on the floor turned and looked again.

A loud – oh, it was so loud – scream echoed around the room. And I sighed.

Every single bald head spun round to the doorway.

Tito, who was not a fan of loud noises or eye contact, stared at the crowd, snarling and sniffing with anger. Then, rearing back to stand upright in the smoke, he hit his chest and roared. So much for sneaking. I think the best way to describe what followed would be: absolute carnage. Chaos. Pure gorilla mayhem.

Chapter 9

A Long Way Down

At the time, I didn't give it much thought. But the more I'd learned about the star swimmers, the dodgier they seemed. Trapping children in rat minds, *forever*, as a punishment? That's got to be illegal. Actually, it probably isn't. Why would anyone write that law? It's definitely wrong though.

Another question was – and this sounds like something my mum might say – why weren't these kids in school? They're all here, learning to be mind jumpers. Like, where are *their* parents? The Whispered Manor was full of pigeons, bald children and questions.

But none of that mattered more than the mission.

What if I lost the ability like Carlos? What if I got trapped?

So what was the plan? Oh yeah, that's right. Run upstairs into Cold Rain's room, find that cell and rescue myself. Easy.

Well, it would have been, but the gorilla was going absolutely bananas.

Everyone seemed to run and scatter, shouting, screaming, panicking. Tito grabbed the bottom of the entire wall of birdcages, lifted it and tipped it over. A hundred pigeons escaped at once. Yep, it's safe to say the relaxing atmosphere was now well and truly disturbed.

Within this madness, I ducked past Tito into the hall, turned for the stairs and was knocked off my feet by a hard leather shoulder. That was the problem with being in a half-starved body. Carlos was nice and all, but man was he weak. Must have weighed less than, I don't know, a bag of walnuts. That's a weird thing to compare it to, sorry. He was skinny, that'll do.

'Oi, watch out, sonny jimbob,' Detective Pepper said.

Amy was by his side, Silent Cameraman filming them both.

'It's me,' I said, clambering back to my feet. 'It's me, Chester.'

'You wot? This is your body? Cos no offence, chief, but I preferred the gorilla. I could snap ya like a warm KitKat. You need a sandwich – what's ya favourite filling eh? I like blue cheese and yella jam, dipped in a sweet cuppa coffee.'

'No, you ... no ... This isn't *my* body, this is Carlos's body. And, *what*, that snack sounds *horrible*.'

'Who's Carlos?' Amy shouted over the noise.

Kids in white robes were barging past, shoving and running – most seem too scared to notice us.

'My friend. He's a rat. Look, it's a long story all right. Why is Tito in here? What happened to the plan?'

A pigeon cage flew over our heads. We all ducked as it exploded on the wall.

'Cor. Let him out the car for a whiz innit,' Detective Pepper said, standing up straight again. 'Greedy sausage got a whiff of the food from the kitchen – does smell naughty to be fair. Smashed the gate open, bolted for the door. Classic silverback.'

Tito picked up a tall teenager and threw him at

a group of adults, who caught him somehow – all knocked to the floor like bowling pins.

'Nah, nah, nah, this is getting out of hand.'

'Listen, my body is upstairs in Cold Rain's room,' I said. 'Maybe this is a good thing – Tito is very distracting. I'm gonna head up there – you sort all this out.'

'Aye aye, laddie. I'll give him a li'l' cuddle. That oughtta calm him down. Gorillas love cuddles.'

Detective Pepper strutted confidently towards Tito and, I presumed, his death. Amy followed and, unsurprisingly, Silent Cameraman was keen to film it.

I found the stairwell and ran, then jogged, then walked up to the top floor. I was panting like crazy when I arrived. There was a door at the end. I pushed it open and stepped inside.

It was cold, slightly blue in there, lit by the faint glow of the moon from the open window. A bookshelf ran all the way round the circular room. In the middle there was a huge table with a leather journal resting on top of it. There was something eerie about this place – like it was from another time. No electricity, no light bulbs, just a cool breeze from the night sky. One shelf on the left had hundreds of ornaments, golden statues and rubies and treasure and other mystical stuff. Weirdly, it was familiar. Maybe it reminded me of a film I'd seen, a fantasy or . . . I don't know. A dream maybe?

Then I thought that perhaps I could steal something. Why not? Cold Rain was definitely a bad guy. Maybe he deserved it. No. See, there it is again, that voice. Stealing things is not OK. Could just steal *one* thing. No, I was getting distracted.

Of course I was curious about all this, but my sights were still set firmly on finding my body. Opposite me, I saw another wooden door.

This was it, the last place it could be. I had reached the top of this tower, the heart of this mad place. It was time to end it.

I stepped towards the door, grabbed the handle, but stopped dead when I heard something.

Scrunching my face, I turned to see a black figure standing behind me. Against the open window he was just a silhouette over the stars. But I could see he was holding a sword.

134

'What are you doing in my room, Carlos?'

I felt slightly embarrassed, like I'd been caught doing something wrong. I guess in a way I had – this was Cold Rain's private quarters. But it was totally justified. *He* was the one who should feel bad. He'd stolen my body.

'Your crimes end here,' he said. 'You have brought shame enough to the order.' Cold Rain walked forwards, out from the slight blue haze of the moon, and struck a match. Now I could see his face and his long black plaited hair clearly in the glowing red candlelight. He lifted the match to his lips and, with a quick puff, blew it out. 'I permit last words, but make them swift, Carlos, for your head must roll this night.'

'A sword?' I said. 'What the hell is this? Grow up.'

'A poor choice. Goodbye.'

Cold Rain spun round and swung his katana right at my face. I ducked just in time, feeling a whistle of air across my scalp.

'Whoa, man, seriously,' I said, touching my head. 'Chill out.' I held up my bony hands and stepped backwards. 'Look, listen, Cold … Mr Rain, I am not actually Carlos.'

'You continue to speak as though the bells of your demise beckon you not. You are Carlos, but not for long.'

'Wait, I thought star swimmers didn't have names?'

'You were exiled to a more fitting creature, *boy* – you are a brother no more.'

He swiped his blade through the air again. I heard the tip hiss like a whip.

I leapt back, bumping into the bookshelf. 'Wait.'

But he drove the sword towards me, showing his teeth and grunting – I fell sideways and it stabbed straight into the wood.

'Please, Mr Rain,' I shouted. 'You're being unreasonable.'

A faint roar echoed from somewhere in the building.

'You summon jungle beasts to do your bidding – it is you, not I, that holds a slender grip on reason.'

'Sorry, yeah, the gorilla thing is my fault. But listen, I'm an eleven-year-old kid. My name is Chester

Parsons. I am here to get my body back. We don't need to be silly about it.'

He frowned, slowly pulling the blade out of the bookshelf. 'Speak again the name you claim to be yours.'

'Chester. Chester Parsons.'

Cold Rain strode past, swaying his sword like he was painting with it – the metal glistened orange and silver in the candlelight. He kept circling me – I turned and turned on the spot to face him.

'You take me for a fool,' he said. 'Am I to believe you are child-actor Chester Parsons on your word alone? Extraordinary claims require extraordinary evidence.'

I smiled. (Yeah, I was pleased he had heard of me – so what?)

'I mean ... sure, happily,' I said. 'But how could I prove it?'

He stopped and pointed the sword at my face. 'Sing the song of the Puff Puff Wheat Puffs.'

'Aw ... really?'

'Serenade the stars or die, sir!'

'Put a little smile on the—'

'No, SING!' He stamped his foot. 'Move. Dance. Tell a story with your body.'

'*Put a little smile on the Puff Puff Wheat Puff*,' I sang, jiggling slightly from side to side. '*A bowl of sunshine, a bowl of fun. A bowl of smiles for everyone. I say, yum-yum puff-puff. One more time it's a yum-yum puff-puff*.'

'Again!'

I repeated the performance, now kind of whimpering with fear.

'You could have heard that tune sung at any tavern, on any moon. This proves nothing. But if your petty games will sow the seeds of a quick death, I shall play them also. I know not of Chester Parsons' body.'

'What? You mean the star swimmers *haven't* kidnapped me?'

'Why would we do such a thing?'

'Because of *Amy and Chester* ... I pretty much spilled the beans on mind jumping.'

Cold Rain blinked, then tried to hide a smile. And then he yelled with laughter. 'Sir, this show is of such poor quality, should anyone have the misfortune of enduring it they would take the claims of animal control to be that of lies. Jest. The work of smoke and trickery. We do not fear such exposure. Certainly not from such a pathetic programme.'

'All right, it's not *that* bad,' I said. 'Didn't you like the swan bit?'

'Fine. I'll concede, that part *was* funny. But that was the *only* good scene in the entire six sorry episodes. Believe it or not, I am somewhat of a television connoisseur. Mark my words, that show will be cast into the abyss of obscurity. Just. Like. You.'

The sword swished my way again. I dodged it. 'Dude. *Stop.*'

I bolted for the other door and barged it open. A cell. A bed. A shelf. A bucket. Some candles. But nothing else. No sleeping Chester. Maybe he was telling the truth – maybe it really wasn't here. I swung round and faced him. If I couldn't jump into my body, I would jump into *his*. But, somehow, I could feel his mind was locked.

'*Please*,' he said, coming towards me again.

This guy is actually going to kill me, I thought,

running out of ideas. If my body *wasn't* here, then where the hell was it?

'Tell me about . . . tell me about Red Fire and Wise Earth,' I blurted – just trying to buy time really.

'You wish to learn the truth? There's the journal you're so desperate to read. Help yourself.'

The leather-bound book was on the table next to the candle – it was just like the one we found in our loft only it was covered in dust. Clearly no one had touched it for years. He smiled when I looked at it. There were answers inside. There had to be. Somehow this was all connected. To me, to my dad, to Dr Vladovski. To my missing body.

Without thinking, I dived for the journal, screaming as the sword slammed down into the table, slicing near my wrist. 'Aw, you're a maniac,' I said, clutching the book under my arm.

As he started slashing at me again, I scrambled through the window, clambering over the balcony railing. He sighed, and calmly followed. Now outside, I climbed up the steep slope of the black slate roof. The old tiles clattered under my feet – one of them came loose, slid and disappeared over the edge. I didn't hear it hit the ground, that's how high it was. Holding the book to my chest, I grabbed a brick chimney pot and looked for somewhere to go. I could see for miles – I could see the perimeter wall, the sprawling land, the trees, the stars, the moon, the distant lights on the horizon.

Then I slid down the other side of the roof, bouncing on Carlos's bony behind, landing on a flat section. I turned and searched, but it was a dead end. There was simply nowhere left to go. I stepped to the edge, leant carefully over and felt instantly sick.

The tower was ridiculously tall. Dizzy, dizzy – no, concentrate.

Maybe there's some guttering or—

'You appear to have depleted your reserves of roof, Carlos,' Cold Rain said, striding towards me, his sword pointed at the ground.

I faced him, my back to the fall. The wind, cold on Carlos's bald head, whipped my white robe around my ankles.

'Now pass me the book.'

I looked down at it. Somehow, in my heart, in

Carlos's heart, I *knew* I needed Wise Earth's journal. I didn't know why, but my instincts were screaming at me, *don't give it to him.*

Although there was no real plan, I decided handing it over wasn't an option. I held the book for him to take. But, as he reached forwards, I snatched it back and threw it over my shoulder. It disappeared, spinning over the edge and, like the tile, we didn't hear it land.

'Whoops,' I said.

He tilted his head and held up his sword. 'Defiance matters not. The wolf eats the brave lambs first.'

'Why do you speak like that?' I said. 'This is all so strange. This situation. This is not normal by today's standards. People just don't behave like this.'

His long black robe stretched out at his side, rippling like a flag, dragged by the wind.

'The truth is – I killed Red Fire,' he said, raising his voice over the weather. 'Wise Earth . . . well, he escaped my wrath and disappeared long ago. He deserted the star swimmers. It seemed right that he should take the blame. I suspect he too is long dead. Should you meet him on the other side, do send him my regards . . .'

Then he gently placed the tip of his sword on my chest and pushed it against me. Not enough to cut, but plenty to knock my balance. My tiptoes were the only thing on the edge of the roof. My back arched, my arms flailed and swung round in big desperate circles, but it was too late. I turned – there was nothing to grab.

And I fell.

Screaming silent nightmare screams I fell and fell. The ground roared towards me, the orange windows of the tower zipping past, like windows on a train that isn't stopping at this station. Stone steps, the building black and blue in the moonlight and the wind howling past. I was falling for the blink of an eye, enough time to spin and realise I was falling head first. The stones rushing up and up and a tiny brown shadow and—

THUD.

Chapter 10

Smashed Potato

It made a sort of FFFF-DUUMMMM sound. Carlos cracked into the ground, bouncing slightly, throwing up gravel and dust from the impact. And yet, no pain. I wasn't dead. In fact, I was conscious, I was alive. I was on the ground, sure, but I wasn't Carlos any more. I was . . .

I take it your body wasn't up there? I heard him think.

Aw, thank you, thank you, I thought. Right place right time, man.

I looked down at the scraggy brown fur and squeaked. I'd never been so happy to be in a rat. I could have kissed that manky thing.

How did you manage to jump? While falling? That . . . that was amazing. What a shot.

Um … I … I don't know, I thought. I just kind of did it. Like a reflex. Like when you blink. It just happened.

So it's true … You must be a Daahsuti master … A prodigy.

Yeah, I guess so.

Nearby, I could see the body I'd just vacated – the head was on backwards, the legs were somewhere near the shoulders – it was all wrong. It looked like an old rag doll that had gone through the wash. A real mess. I felt bad.

Dear me. Sorry, Carlos. That is … I mean that really is not cool.

It's fine.

I was taking good care of it, but Cold Rain pushed me.

I told you he was bad news.

But hey, look, I stole the journal.

Near the mangled mass of arms and legs and muddy white robes, the book was lying face down on the grass. We scurried over, bit it, and dragged it to a nearby bush, where we pushed it right against the side of the building, making sure it was properly hidden.

I think we need to speak to the police, I thought. I am pretty sure that was a murder.

Honestly, Chester, don't worry about it. Body wasn't great anyway. Creaky knees, wonky nose. Besides, I had no use for it any more.

Still, pushing people off roofs is not OK.

Carlos was being incredibly reasonable about all this. I wouldn't have taken it quite so well if he'd ruined *my* body. Aw, I really do miss it. Even that weird mole I have on my leg. Even the strange whistle my nose does every now and then. Even when it catches a cold, even when it makes weird smells, even when it moves wrong and I bump my head or stub my toe. I still love it because it's *mine*. It's *my* silly sack of squishy meat and clumsy bones.

We nestled deep in the bush. Now I could smell the mud and, *sniff-sniff-sniff*, the dinner from the Whispered Manor kitchen. I guess they were cooking for loads of people.

How many star swimmers are there? I wondered.

What's a ...? Oh yeah. Globally a few thousand. Here only about two hundred.

Need to find Tito, I thought. And hey, you were right by the way – Cold Rain said *he* killed Red Fire. He blamed it on Wise Earth.

I knew that story didn't add up.

But he said Wise Earth went missing – do you reckon *he* stole my body?

It is possible. Yes. But finding him probably isn't. He hasn't been seen for ages.

Have you got any idea where we should start looking? What do you know about him?

Wise Earth founded the star swimmers about nine hundred and ninety years ago. So as you might have guessed, he's pretty old.

How is that even possible? A human body can't live that long, no matter how much you meditate.

You're right, Carlos thought. *One human can't live that long. But I never said he used the same body. This is what Daahsuti elders do.*

What do you mean?

So when they get old, they go to hospital right?

Sure.

And what happens in hospitals?

Loads of stuff. They heal people, do surgery, X-rays ... alcohol gel ... beds on wheels ... expensive car parks?

Know what the maternity ward does?

Takes care of women having babies?

Bingo.

Wait, they mind jump into babies?

That's right. They can live forever. Once your body gets too old, just get an upgrade. Like a mobile phone.

Well, it's not quite the same but ... yeah ... I see what you mean. Surely this is wrong though? Stealing a baby's body? Do the parents know?

What do you think? Of course not.

And then, what, they bring the kids here and retrain them?

Exactly. Some time after their eighth birthday – before that they're hard to teach. I was ten when I arrived.

But ... that's kidnapping ... it's illegal ... How do they get away with it?

The children want to come. Or at least they think they do ...

What do the parents say?

Nothing ... These elders, they have the power to change anyone's mind. To make them forget. To make them agree to anything. That's sort of the main point of the star swimmers. Controlling people is what it's all about.

And the kids themselves? Can they remember it all?

With help, and guidance, yes.

So Wise Earth must have done it loads?

Yes, about fourteen times I think. Makes an average of a new body every seventy-ish years.

What does his latest one look like?

He's fairly old now – grey hair, in a long plait. Black robe. Can't miss him. As for where he might be, that's a different matter.

I'm guessing this journal will have answers. We need to find Amy and Detective Pepper too – it'll take us ages to read this book with stupid little rat hands.

I thought again about Carlos's human body.

Look, I meant what I thought earlier. I want you to come live with us. It's the least I can do. We'll get a wheel, cool cage, everything. You'll be the happiest rat in town. We need a new pet anyway. Our dog died.

Aw no, how?

Well, I left— sorry, MY SISTER left the garden gate open and she ran away.

Shame, what was her name?

D . . . um . . . Da . . . Dummm . . . I . . . I can't remember.

I really *couldn't* remember. This was a horrible feeling. I know my dead dog's name. I know this. Come on. Daaaah . . .

Uh-oh, Carlos thought. *Not a good sign.*

What . . . Why?

You're forgetting. Pretty soon you'll forget how to mind jump, then you'll stop being Chester altogether. You're smoke in a breeze, a morning fog, a melting flake of late winter snow. There, and then not.

All right. OK. OK. So we have to be fast – I get it. But, wait, what about your memories?

How do you mean?

Don't they live in your brain? Like a computer's hard drive?

It's possible, yes. What's your point?

Well, your brain is clearly smashed to a pulp.

It's what?!

We looked out through the dark swaying leaves and twigs at Carlos's body on the broken stone path.

Oh yeah, of course. I guess memories are strange?

Also, I was wondering, why do you think sometimes I can mind jump so easily, and other times I can't do it at all?

It depends partly on your body. If it's relaxed, in a trance, you can do it – if it's disturbed, you can't. That's why you make sure you leave it somewhere safe, like in bed.

Hey, look who it is . . .

Cold Rain appeared at the front door. He strode over to Carlos's body, laughed, then started searching for the journal. We were perched on top of it, safely hidden in the gloomy undergrowth. Brown rat on a brown book – great camouflage. After a while a young star swimmer came outside and stood behind him.

'Lord Rain, we have a problem.'

Pfft, Lord Rain, I thought. Losers.

'Indeed, brother, we do,' Cold Rain said. 'Wise Earth's journal has gone missing. The man who has taken it will meet a fate worse than Carlos. Find the book.'

'Certainly,' the man said, with a bow. 'But you are needed in the kitchen – we've managed to lock the gorilla in the pantry. However, its mind is relatively advanced. We need an elder to escort it away from the manor.'

'I care not for such distractions,' Cold Rain said, crouching and checking around the path for clues. He picked some grass and sniffed it, then squinted. 'If you cannot tame the beast, I suggest you kill it.'

This guy sucks, I thought. Right, let's leave the journal here and go save Tito. Can you get us into the pantry?

Chester, I'm a rat. Getting into the pantry is my speciality.

We scurried round the back of the building, staying hidden in the shadows – only patches of grey moonlight and cats could find us now. Luckily there didn't seem to be any cats about. Being a rodent is ridiculously stressful – so many things are trying to kill you. Even owls. When you're a human, owls seem so friendly, but they're really not. They're terrible. Three-hundred-and-sixty-degree, telescopic night vision, perfect hearing, stealth wings, razor-sharp claws and, if that's not scary enough, they can *fly*. But you won't see them coming. You'll just be chilling out in the grass, maybe humming a little rat tune to yourself and then BAM. They swoop down, grab you in their talons, literally rip you to pieces with their hooked beak, eat *everything*, then cough up the fur and bones and teeth in neat little pellets. Don't let all that 'Whooo, whooo, whoooooo' stuff fool you. Owls are wrong. Owls are actual monsters.

Why do people think nature is nice when, clearly, it's completely horrible?

Anyway, I could smell the food more and more as we got closer to the kitchen. No wonder Tito had been tempted by this – it smelled amazing. The rat in us was getting excited – I felt its nose twitch and its tiny stomach grumble.

Beneath a glowing window, we approached the dark stone bricks. There was a tiny black crack near the ground and a narrow tunnel had been dug in the dry earth.

We squeezed through the gap, *sniff-sniff-sniffing* the warm air in front of us. It took a real wiggle to crawl inside but, with a final push, we arrived in a dark cave of foody wonders. Huge sacks of potatoes and cereal and chocolate and bread and hundreds of jars filled with all sorts. So much food. So much temptation – I felt my little body shaking with excitement.

This rat needs to calm down, I thought.

Nah, that's me. I love breaking into the pantry. Let me show you the secret biscuits.

No. We're here for Tito.

Aw, but . . .

Biscuits later.

We scampered towards the light and, from under the wooden shelf, saw a huge black mass of fur – Tito's thigh. He was sitting on the reddish tiles of the pantry floor. We crawled out and stared up.

At first I was worried. Maybe they had hurt him? I still felt responsible for the gorilla – he was, after all, kind of mine.

You said you stole him from the zoo?

That was narration, Carlos, I wasn't speaking to you.

Well, who were you speaking to?

The . . . the reader . . . I'm telling a story.

Uh-oh, you're losing your mind . . .

No. This is . . . Stop making me doubt myself.

Either way, he looks fine to me.

Carlos was right. In fact, I'd never seen a happier animal in my life.

Tito was slouched on the ground, leaning against the shelves. He was surrounded by countless wrappers and half-eaten fruit and vegetables and jars of this and that. There was jam on the floor, broken crackers, thousands of grains of rice and dented tins. He'd had a feast. His stomach was bulging and his breathing sounded almost like he was asleep – like he was snoring.

Then we spotted the bottles.

Is that . . .? Is that wine?

A deep gorilla burp echoed in the pantry.

That, Carlos thought, *is not a good smell.*

Tito's eyes were half closed and his head looked too

155

heavy for him to hold up. He hiccupped and grunted. Hiccupped and grunted.

Right, Carlos, I'll speak to you soon, I thought, as I lined us up and stared at Tito.

The sound of mind jumping was, now I think about it, a bit like the wind when I was falling earlier. A quick whistling whoosh and then bam. Done. Just like that I was back in Tito's mind. In a strange way, it felt like home. Which was comforting *and* terrifying.

Now my vision was blurry, I had peanut butter all over my left hand and an empty wine bottle in my right. Look at the state of this, I thought. I frowned down at Carlos – I could see two of him. Two small brown rats waving at me. Double gorilla vision. Swaying, I threw the bottle – it smashed on the back of the pantry door.

'He's getting angry again,' a voice from the other side yelled. Then the door opened quickly and another bottle of red wine rolled inside and stopped at my hairy knee. Carlos sniffed it.

They were getting Tito drunk. This was probably cruel. I admit it was less cruel than killing him like

Cold Rain suggested. But still. I mean, it was funny too, don't get me wrong, but this was a cult of *mind jumpers*. Surely they could figure out a way to get rid of a gorilla? Maybe they were softening him up with wine first. Not on my watch.

I carefully reached down, picked up Carlos and let him scurry along my tree-trunk arm and perch on my shoulder. To him I must have seemed gigantic.

Right. It was time to leave. I stood, pressed my fists into the floor and got my balance straight. Then I dragged out a huge sack of potatoes.

These star swimmers were in every flavour of trouble now. I counted backwards, three ... two ... one.

I took a breath, then leapt forwards, ripping the door from its hinges and slamming it flat on to the ground like a matching card in a game of snap.

BANG. SNAP. WHAT'S ALL THIS?

The sight of a drunk silverback gorilla with a rat on its shoulder must have been shocking because the people in the kitchen just stared at me. There were three star swimmers – bald, white robes and scared faces. They were all just standing there. Stunned. No one knew what to do.

But then one of them stepped forwards and hit me over the head with a broom.

'Urrgh.'

It was more annoying than painful. I turned to him, swaying a little. He looked truly sorry.

'*Nice* gorilla,' he whispered, holding up his hands.

Leaning sideways, I drew the sack of potatoes behind me like it was a baseball bat. Then, with a grunt, I swung it with everything I had. GRRR-BOOOF.

The man went flying across the huge kitchen, over the counter, knocking pots and pans and plates and thudding to a stop against the wall.

Another incredibly brave (stupid) one came forwards, so he also got dealt a powerful potato blow and off he went, spinning in a blur of white robes. I laughed – hahahargh – and heard a squeak of satisfaction by my ear. Tito was so outrageously strong – it was such an unfair fight. Also, I think alcohol makes gorillas more aggressive than normal, which is why this potato violence felt . . . well . . . it just felt *right*. Besides, it was self-defence. They started it.

The third and final guy stood in my way, holding a

knife. *A knife.* Surely he'd run away, I thought. And yet he didn't. I looked down at him, frowned and slowly shook my head. He was shivering with terror and, after a couple of seconds, the knife fell to the floor, bouncing on the tiles.

Then he stared back into my eyes, squinted and rubbed his temples. Ha. He was trying to mind jump into me. I guess you have to respect him for trying. There was a slight tingle on my forehead. It gave me goosebumps, the fur on my neck standing on end. So this is what it feels like, I thought. However, I could tell, as he was young and not particularly relaxed, that he didn't stand a chance of breaking in.

But still, he was in my path. So I grabbed him by the scruff of his robe, pulled him close to my face and yelled, 'GOOOOAAAH AAAAHHWAAAY!' as loud as I could. Which is very, very loud.

And he fainted. Just turned to jelly in my hands. The little loser. I frowned. I was sort of annoyed. I wanted him to attack me so I had an excuse to throw him or dip him in the soup or whack him with the potatoes. Grunting, I gave him a shake. His head just jiggled and lolled about. Out cold. Seemed unfair to chuck him around now, so I just placed him carefully on the kitchen floor and patted him on the cheek.

The other two had got to their feet and, sensibly, limped away.

Stumbling against the wall for balance, I strode over to the tall fridge, grabbed the door but, instead of faffing about with the handle, I just slammed the whole thing on to its side. Milk, old salad leaves, a half-eaten chicken, broken eggs, all strewn across the tiles. Looked like the fridge had been sick. I reached inside and grabbed a wedge of cheese, took a bite, then rested it on my shoulder for Carlos.

I heard more of them outside the kitchen. Instead of fighting (which was tempting), I decided to leave via a large hole in the wall which was conveniently there after I threw the fridge at it a couple of times.

Back outside in the chilly night, I went round the side of the building to the bush. I leant low, reached inside and found Wise Earth's journal. Holding it tight to my chest I ran back down the path towards the gate on my three remaining limbs.

'There you are,' Amy said, walking out from behind a tree. I skidded to a stop. 'I take it that's you, Chester? Hey, cool rat.'

'Carlos, eeergh is Ameh. Ameh, eeergh is Carlos.'

She looked closely at the rat on my shoulder, then at the book under my arm. 'Oh good, you've found Wise Earth's journal.'

I nodded, holding it out for her. Then I froze.

Wait.

How did Amy know about the book?

She grabbed it, but I didn't let go – she pulled, but I held it in place.

I glanced around for Detective Pepper and Silent Cameraman. But no. Amy was all alone. We just stared into each other's eyes. Then, spinning like a grey leaf, a wispy pigeon feather fell slowly out of the tree behind her.

'Give me the book, brave little lamb,' she whispered.

Chapter 11

Where is Wise Earth?

This was getting out of hand. I was finding it hard enough keeping track of who *I* was – one minute I'm a rat, the next I'm a skinny teenage boy, then I'm a boozy gorilla. But now I had to deal with this too?

Standing under that tree in the Whispered Manor garden, in the shaded moonlight that made green things grey and grey things black, I could tell Amy wasn't herself. This wasn't Just Amy. This wasn't Loser Amy. This was Completely New Amy, a.k.a. Cold Rain – the cheeky freak wasn't even trying to hide in her mind.

Carlos squeaked on my shoulder – even he could tell something was wrong.

Seeing someone else control my sister was obviously creepy, but it also made me feel guilty about the times *I* had trespassed in her brain. It feels so weird having another consciousness thinking alongside yours – even someone cool like Carlos. But I can't imagine how terrible it must be if you don't want it to happen. Worse than someone reading your diary, or snooping through your phone. Thoughts are the one thing that should always be private.

Mind jumping is really dodgy. It's not a game. Why didn't someone warn me?

'Listen, boy,' Completely New Amy said. 'It would be a shame if anything were to happen to me, don't you think? An accident say? I could fall off something high, or perhaps trip on to the point of a sword?'

I grunted.

We were both still holding the journal. Tito and Amy face to face, neither one themselves.

Then I felt that familiar tingle at the front of my head – Cold Rain was trying to access the gorilla's mind. It was like the star swimmer's attempt in the kitchen, just a million times stronger. Still, I managed to resist. It's almost impossible to describe this sensation – it's a bit like the feeling when you're straining to remember something, combined with that fuzzy head rush after you stand up too fast. You can kind of sense a slight presence pressing against your thoughts and you know, if you relax, it'll get inside. It requires a lot of concentration to keep a good mind jumper out.

Amy sighed and the tingle disappeared. 'Well played,' she said. 'As strong as your current form suggests. How interesting ... I would remark upon this, but I know not of an adage for the stubborn lamb. What possible answers do you seek within those pages?' She let go of the book. 'Read it. Go on. If your heart beats hard for truth and soft for life, then peruse the words. It matters not to me.'

Was this a trick? All this hassle and now Cold Rain was just giving up?

Hesitating, but only once, I opened the book.

And all the pages were blank.

'Wheeaargh?!' I said, flicking through with my huge black thumbs.

There was just one single line on the first page, written in perfect cursive writing. Old-fashioned, the curly kind you write with one of those feathery fountain pen things. What are they called? A . . . a . . . qu . . .

'Keep this journal,' I read. 'I will return to fill it with tales of redemption. And be warned, brother, I shall use your blood for ink if the grave is yet to claim you.'

Then it was signed, 'Wise Earth'.

Confused, frustrated, I groaned and threw the book on the grass. All this for a short, meaningless message? This didn't explain anything. This was just—

A quill. Ah, yeah, that's it.

Completely New Amy picked the journal up off the ground, clutched it to her chest and walked back to the Whispered Manor. I watched her go, looking back up the front of that huge building with its tall spiked spires and glowing orange windows. The bricks seemed black now, fading out and up to nothing in the night sky. And above I noticed the stars – more than I had ever seen before. So many that, in some patches, they were like fog, like a cloud of glitter flicked across a ceiling that isn't even there. I turned full circle, space arching over us, reflected perfectly in Carlos's brown eyes. And the rat blinked. Even with all the anger and mystery, the trouble and sadness, a trillion stars continued to burn in peace.

In our third session, Dr Vladovski had asked me why the universe is beautiful. When I shrugged, he whispered, 'The universe is beautiful because we can see it.'

I think I get what he meant now.

Amy went to the front door and posted the book through the letter box, then she strolled back down the path and stood next to the tree again.

'I believe you to be, as you claim, Chester Parsons,' Cold Rain said through her mouth. 'You have a gift to which I must show respect, a talent of wonder and art. But even those as skilled as us should not linger away from ourselves too long.'

Tito's heart was pumping – we were scared. I'd put all my hope in finding my body here. Now it felt like I was lost, like I was back to square one.

'Wheergh is hee?' I asked.

'I do not know where Wise Earth is. Nor would I tell you if I did. And do not underestimate his ability to hide – he moves by shadow, he sings by silence, he swims by the stars in our night.'

I rolled my eyes.

'Although, I shall say this. If he lives to this day and you *do* meet with him, I suspect you will find answers too. Endless wisdom awaits those who ask the right questions.'

Grunting again, I closed my eyes. I wish these people could just speak normally.

'I hold the journal in anticipation, in whispered hope that he will keep his word and return,' she said. 'But perhaps I dare dream too far. Maybe he is truly gone.'

A plan came to me. An idea.

'Wheregh did he live?' I said. 'Afteeerh he left staarrh swimmerghs?'

Cold Rain wasn't going to help me, that was obvious, but if I could get him to at least *think* about Wise Earth, Amy might see it too. That's the thing with consciousness. Thoughts come into your mind – they just appear, as if from nowhere. But you can affect it with words, sounds, pictures. We can't help ourselves. If someone says, 'Imagine the smell of warm popcorn,' it's quite likely you will. Vladovski even said, 'You stand a better chance of authoring the thoughts of another than you do your own.'

So perhaps I couldn't control what appeared in *my* mind, but maybe I could control what appeared in Amy's. I sensed Cold Rain in there, behind her eyes, staring at me. And I could see it working.

'The sand falls fast, the sun draws long, the clock spins and spins,' she whispered, blinking as though she was tired. 'Tick . . . tock . . . Tick . . . tock . . . Be kind to your sister, Chester. I can feel she loves you very much.'

And with that, Cold Rain looked up at the pigeon in the tree above. Amy gasped and grabbed her forehead as he left. The bird shuffled, leapt from the branch and flew straight back up to the Whispered Manor, beneath the stars.

'Wot's going on then?' Detective Pepper asked. 'Eh?'

'Shush,' Amy snapped. 'Just be quiet.'

She was sitting on the bonnet of the car. We had parked in a lay-by about a mile away, on a winding road that zigzagged up the side of a hill. From here, through the trees, across the horizon, I saw the Whispered Manor below. At this distance you could never guess what went on inside that place.

'Nice view,' Detective Pepper said.

My plan worked – *kind of*.

'I... I heard him... I felt him thinking in my mind,' Amy had said. 'I... I saw a place. It's hazy... I... Wise Earth and Cold Rain. They were there together. They were arguing. Fighting about something.'

The image she had was clear – she described the place we needed to go. But she couldn't tell us *where* it actually was. Now Amy was desperately trying to remember. Trying to remember someone else's memories.

'They used to be friends,' she whispered. 'Aw, it's right there, like a name you know but can't recall. They were... they were having dinner. I...' She wrapped her arms around her head and scrunched her eyes.

'Hang about, I got an idea,' Detective Pepper said.

'Will you *please* be quiet.'

'Nah, listen. He pictured something using your noggin, right? What if there's more information in there. Like a' internet cookie on a computer – remembers ya password and that. What if you trigger something. Specific like.'

The gravel on the ground crunched under my fist as I came closer, behind the car and on to the edge of the road. 'What are you saying?' I typed.

'Lemme tell ya a story.' Detective Pepper turned to me, Amy and Silent Cameraman, making sure we were all paying attention. 'It's my fourth birthday. We got cake. Jam. Buttercream. Very nice. Very nice indeed. But we also got a big bowl o' jelly. Lemon flavour. Yella.'

'This *better* be going somewhere,' Amy said.

'I'm sitting at the table, mouth fulla jelly. Havin' a lovely time. My brother, now he was a naughty little scamp. Mean. I tell ya. Used to throw rocks at me. Once he stole my pencil case and replaced all the pens with worms. Cold wet worms. I open it up in class – teacher sees, shows everyone. From that day on they called me The Worminator.'

'What's the point of this story?!'

'Hang about, we're getting there. Back to the birthday. I'm eating jelly. And my brother, he gets one of the candles, lights it, then ... cor ... then he comes over and drips hot wax down the back of my neck. I'm screaming, I'm crying. It hurts. Parents, well, they was proper angry ... tea party was ruined. Now, to this day, if I see lemon jelly, if I smell it, even if I think about the stuff, I remember that moment vividly. Just sails me back there, every time. Connected, ya know, been conditioned to associate lemon jelly with pain.'

Amy was nodding.

'Now.' Detective Pepper faced her. 'You said Wise matey and Rainy chops were eating dinner together. What were they havin'?'

'Um ...' She closed her eyes. 'Italian food ...'

'Gotta be specific.'

'Uh ... there was spaghetti and ...' She looked up. 'Olives. They were eating olives.'

'Right. Oi.' Detective Pepper clicked his fingers at Silent Cameraman. 'Gimme some olives.'

Silent Cameraman just shrugged.

'We'll go buy some.'

'It's the middle of the night,' Amy said. 'Shops are closed.'

'I know – we'll get Brian on the blower.' Detective Pepper took his phone from his pocket, went to his contacts and pressed call. 'Tell him we need some olives, pronto.' He held the mobile to his ear.

While we waited on the side of the road, I sat in the lay-by and let Carlos crawl up and down my arm. When he arrived at my hand, I threw him into the air and he landed on my head. Squeaking, he nodded for me to do it again. Teaching my new pet rat tricks would, normally, be fun – Carlos was certainly enjoying it. But my thoughts kept drifting. I would be worrying about my body, about finding Wise Earth, about getting answers, and then I'd start daydreaming about food and the jungle. I'd flinch and then realise where I was – stay focused, I thought. Don't get lost.

Also we checked the news and the zoo people had sent out an emergency response team. Which was bad. As far as they were concerned, they had a missing gorilla. I don't know much about running a zoo but I bet losing a dangerous animal is one of the worst things that can happen. Obviously I would have returned Tito but I needed a mind for my consciousness to live in – no way would Amy let me shack up with her until I found my body. And being in Detective Pepper's brain? No thank you.

Some time later a car came up the road, its headlights stinging my eyes.

Brian pulled into the lay-by with new batteries for the camera and a bag of snacks.

'I had black olives in the fridge and found this jar of green ones in the back of the cupboard,' he said, closing the driver's door.

'Aw, chief, you are a diamond.' Detective Pepper lifted out a couple of plastic pots. 'Amy, throw a few of these down ya shouter. Give 'em a sniff. If they don't trigger something then nothing will. Taste 'n smell – early senses, ya know, get bonded right tight to memories. Top job, Brian, top job.'

He was right, Brian *was* brilliant. We didn't even have to explain why we needed the olives. Once he understood that it was important, he drove out here to help us – no questions asked. Still, we explained everything to him and he seemed even more concerned than before.

'Chest-o,' he said, sitting carefully on the ground by my side, putting his arm round my hairy shoulder. 'It's going to be OK, yah? You hang in there, all right?'

I grunted.

Amy took the small olive pots and sat on a tree stump in the entrance to the woods, where it was a little quieter.

'Red Rose Pictures,' Brian added, shaking his head and looking across the road. 'They're furious with me. All I wanted to do was make them … make them proud. Make splendid television. A second series that'd win awards. A second series that'd get viewing figures that meant something.' He sighed. 'All my life I've tried my best. I just … I've produced more than fifty TV shows.' Brian laughed a sad laugh, his shoulders hunched over. 'The critics hate them all. They call my work contrived – so I make it natural. Then they call it boring. I can't win. It hurts to pour your heart and soul into a project and get ridiculed.

Laughed at. Considered a joke. Maybe my best just isn't good enough.'

I patted his thigh – probably too hard, but he appreciated the gesture.

'And now this . . . Now . . .' He stared down into his lap and picked at his fingernail. Brian had bags under his eyes – he was clearly exhausted. And his fake tan made him look worse. All his wrinkles and creases were dark, all his enthusiasm had drained away. 'If anything happens to you, kid . . . it's . . . it's all over.'

I could tell, even though Silent Cameraman was filming this, Brian was being himself. For the first time, I truly wanted to make *Amy and Chester* a success. I decided right there and then that when I found myself, I would try harder – I wouldn't complain, I wouldn't moan. We'd finish the show. And it would be good.

'Brian,' I typed into my machine. 'I know what it feels like to fail. The only people who think I'm a serious actor are my mum and Amy. To everyone else I'm just the kid who can control animals.'

'No, no, don't be silly.' Brian smiled. 'You'll *always* be the Puff Puff Wheat Puffs kid.'

'Harr ... harr.' I faked a laugh.

Sitting on my foot, Carlos began humming the jingle. I grumbled and flicked him off – he rolled across the ground and squeaked to silence.

'But you're so young, Chest-o – so talented, so much potential,' Brian said. 'You've got your whole life ahead of you. Me? I'm in my fifties. I work in TV. Who even watches TV nowadays? Who sits down, flicks on the telly and sees what's on? Nobody, that's who. Those days are long gone. Now, kids, they just stream the best thing, they just log on and enjoy their favourite YouTubers.' He waved towards Amy but she wasn't listening. 'No offence to her, of course, you know I *love* her work. Oh, I'm an old man in a young man's game. This series ... it's the last chance I'm going to get.'

'Oi, that'll do, all right, rein it in a bit yeah?' Detective Pepper said. 'Ya being a right soppy sausage, banging on about ya career. Monkey chops ain't even got a body. He's playin' a game of musical chairs and there ain't no chairs left, ya know. Music's gone. Nowhere to sit.'

'Yah, yah, yes, yes you're right. Of course. This is

not about me.' Brian stood and composed himself. 'I'm sorry. I didn't mean to be insensitive.'

Detective Pepper's headlights were sending white beams into the woods ahead and the hazard lights clunked on then off, on then off, a yellow glow warming up the darkness. Amy was still on the tree stump at the edge of the road. I watched her as she sniffed olives and wrestled with her memories. This was especially nice of her as I knew she absolutely hated olives – she once described them as disgusting salt grapes that taste like coins combined with seawater. I don't mind them but I see what she means.

Amy was sitting perfectly still and every time the hazard lights flashed, she appeared in the yellow light, then disappeared into darkness again. Clunk-clunk, clunk-clunk, clunk-clunk. Amy sitting, pitch-black, Amy sitting, pitch-black, Amy sitting, pitch-black, Amy standing up, pitch-black, Amy turning, pitch-black and then, finally, Amy smiling.

'I know where we need to go,' she whispered from the trees. 'I know where Wise Earth lived.'

Chapter 12

Under the Bed Downtown

'Hey guys,' Amy said as she drove Detective Pepper's car. She was back to her old self. Or her new self. This was Loser Amy speaking to the audience, via Silent Cameraman, who was filming her from the passenger seat. 'So total cray-cray night. In terms of progress it's a five. But if I was scoring it on strangeness . . . defo the *big ten*. Let's run from the top. Number one, Chester's body is not, I repeat *not*, at the Whispered Manor. I know, right?' She made an explosion noise. 'Bombshell. Number two, the rat on Tito's shoulder . . .'

Silent Cameraman swung round to film me. Carlos stood up on his hind legs and bowed.

'That's actually one of the star swimmers. As

a punishment they made him live in a rat's body. Like, forever.'

We drove along a main road. I watched the street lights flow past, the car flashed orange, then dark, orange, then dark, specks of rain glowing on the window. I wanted to smash those street lights, every last one, but I didn't know why.

I was worrying more and more about my memories. What else couldn't I remember? There was no way to tell. It is literally impossible to make a list of things you have forgotten because, well, you've forgotten them. How long did I have left? This was uncharted territory. Like swimming really far out to sea – there will be a point when you don't have enough energy to get back.

And that's the end of you.

How long before I drown in Tito's mind? Drown like Carlos in this rat?

'That is a bit strong innit,' Detective Pepper said. He was sitting in the back with me. 'Now if I had to be an animal for the rest of my life – tough one that – I guess I'd be a . . . a cat maybe? Have a right good snuggle in the sunshine. Terrorise a goldfish and— Nah, nah,

nah, hang about, scratch that one – I'd be a cam-o DOUGH dragon. Done. Sign me up.'

There was a long pause and, when we realised he meant 'Komodo dragon', we all laughed.

'Wot? That's a top choice. You can pipe down 'n all, Carlos, you're a rat, mate.'

'How far away is until we arrive?' I typed into my talky machine thing.

'Doesn't really make sense,' Amy said. 'But I know what you mean. Not long now.'

'I love this motor but sitting in the back ain't my cuppa tea,' Detective Pepper said, shuffling around, his leather jacket squeaking on the leather seats.

'Yeah, well, I need to present the update and I know the way, so you'll have to make do,' Amy said. 'Where was I?' She turned to the camera. 'So, guys, a man called Wise Earth founded the star swimmers like a thousand years ago – and now we're heading to his last known location. Maybe he—'

'I can do all that,' Detective Pepper said. 'Oi, chief, swing that rand this way.' Silent Cameraman pointed the camera into the back of the car. 'That's it. Right—'

'No, I'm doing it,' Amy said.

'Nah, I've got this one, buttercup.' He grabbed the camera so it stayed locked on him. 'You just concentrate on the road. Right, so we're off to this gaff which, according to Amy's nut, is where this wise geezer used to live – he's been missing for ages. Now I've had some cases in my day, but this one is, well, I tell ya... We've got an ancient order that eats babies, right, a bad bunch—'

'Nurgh,' I said.

'Wot?'

Then I typed: 'No, they don't *eat* babies, they *steal* babies. They mind jump into them. When that body gets old they just go down the hospital and get another one – so they can kind of live forever.'

Carlos nodded.

'All right, whatever,' Detective Pepper said. 'I knew a bloke back in the eighties. He had a baby. Full head of hair from day one. Looked like a furry football. Little Darren Baxter. Grew up to be trouble 'n all. That barnet though. Haunts me.'

'See?' Amy said. 'That's why you can't do a piece to camera – you ramble on about nothing.'

'Nah, nah, I was getting to it.'

'Anyway,' she continued, Silent Cameraman focusing on her again, 'with luck we'll find Wise Earth and he'll know something about Chester's body.'

'Wise Earth,' Detective Pepper said. 'Wise. Earth. Mr Earth. Hey, Wise, how was ya weekend? Establish any wonky mystic cults? Hack into any babies? *Wise Earth*. Who'd call themselves that, eh?'

'It doesn't matter,' I typed. 'All we need to do is find him. He's at the centre of this. He's the key.'

'Oi, back here,' Detective Pepper said. Silent Cameraman turned again. 'I'm feelin' sidelined if I'm honest. Monkey chops – top lad, can't fault him. But sometimes that Amy girl is quite spikey. I think she might be jealous. She's threatened by me. She wants the show to be all about her – ya notice how she took all the credit for the olive idea? Gone to her head innit. Bit of a diva, ya know?'

'I *can* hear you,' Amy said.

'Yeah but they'll just edit it later – little talking-head thing. Cut to me having a chinwag. Cut back to you. Maybe we should play on this rivalry? Get a bit of a feud goin', just bants though, above the belt, ya-know-what-I-mean?'

'I think you might be a fruitloop, Mr Pepper,' Amy said. 'Like legit crazy.'

'Nah, I think *you* might be.'

'Hmm, I think you are.'

'Thing is though, Amy, you.'

'You.'

'Nah you.'

I grunted. There was a long silence.

'Your sister, she's hard work ain't she?' Detective Pepper whispered, leaning over to me. 'Looks sweet but give it a poke and it'll get punchy. Like a kangaroo. *Never* poke a kangaroo. One of the first things they teach ya in the army. You ever controlled a kangaroo?'

I wasn't paying attention – I just stared out of the window.

'Oi, monkey chops.'

'You know gorillas aren't actually monkeys,' I typed.

'You wot? Course they are. If … if they ain't monkeys, what are they? Fish? Dogs? Come off it.'

'He's right,' Amy said, checking the wing mirrors. 'Gorillas are apes. They're actually closer to humans than to monkeys.' Just Amy is pretty clever, she knows stuff. 'This is the place,' she whispered, pulling up into a dingy alleyway.

The ground was damp from the drizzle – puddles like black mirrors on the tarmac were exactly the same as the sky above, just darker. (I jumped in a puddle once and it was deeper than my wellies. That used to be what I would call a 'bad day'. Losing your body really puts things into perspective.)

We all climbed out of the car. The building was an old corner shop, gloomy, boarded up and covered in graffiti. It seemed abandoned – looked like a 'proper dodgy little gaff' according to Detective Pepper.

Above the derelict shop was an apartment. 'Up there, that's it,' Amy said. 'This is what Cold Rain remembered. The last time they were together.'

Before we headed inside, Silent Cameraman got some footage of the scene, stepping out into the road to get a better view of the long parade of shops. As he did, Detective Pepper walked across the pavement, made sure he was standing in shot, then popped the collar on his leather jacket.

'Right, let's do it,' he said, pulling on his sleeves. Amy shook her head at the camera.

We found some steel steps around the rear of the building. First up was Silent Cameraman who filmed Amy and Detective Pepper as they raced to the top, jostling for position like children. I came up last, my big fists clonking on each rusting step. I had no idea what time it was, but it was quiet, so we're probably talking after midnight. All I could hear was the odd bit of traffic. I also couldn't see the stars any more, not in the sky above or the puddles below. Nearby street lights had stolen them. Oh yeah, *that's* why I hate street lights – they ruin night-time.

'Hey, looks like someone's beaten us to it,' Amy said, pointing at the door, which had been broken. 'Crowbar maybe?'

She teased it open and went into the dark corridor.

'Oi oi, there she goes,' Detective Pepper whispered. 'Waltzing right past the most obvious piece of evidence I've ever seen in my thirty-five years on this earth.'

Amy turned around and laughed. 'As *if* you're only thirty-five.'

'Easy, tiger sauce, that's my showbiz age, ya know? Maybe it's closer to forty-five. Maybe not. Depends who's askin'.'

'The *evidence*,' Amy snapped. 'What am I meant to have missed?'

'Ah, well, if you don't know then ...'

'Tell uhs,' I grunted.

Detective Pepper leant against the wall by the door, sighing and looking at his fingernails. 'Have a gander at that lock then.'

'Yeah, someone's broken in,' Amy said.

He sighed again. 'Look closer.'

'What? If you're trying to claim credit for spotting it then you can—'

'DAH, dah, dah, dah, dah. It's not a competition, Amy. We're all on the same side.' He crouched down and beckoned Silent Cameraman. 'Zoom in on this business, chief. Whatdyasee, eh? Damage. Scratch marks around the lock. A break-in? Nah if I didn't know better I'd say this was the work of a crowbar.'

'Yeah, I *said* that.'

'Dah, dah.' He held up his hand. 'But. But. BUT . . . the holes are too small. They're making tiny crowbars now are they? Tools for dwarfs? Pull the other one, come on, I wasn't born yesterday – dwarves use normal-size tools. Typically, their hands are deceivingly large. Strong too. I used to work with one. Big Jeff we called him. Cruel nickname really. Nah. This ain't the work of shrunken burglars. This here . . .' He looked right into the camera lens. '*This* was caused by . . . a hook.'

'Hmmm,' I said.

'Bang. Bosh. Bingady ding-dong. Yes. YES.' He stood up and threw his arms into the air. 'He shoots he scores. Back in the game. Just like that, Pepper's headline news again. Front page. Right at the top. They've got a picture. It's an old one. He looks nice.'

'Well done,' Amy said, touching the broken wood. 'I think you might be right.'

'Course I'm right. Nah come on. Amy Scale. Shall we call that a ten?'

'Four.'

'Aw, ya just bein' silly now,' he said. 'That was one

of the best discoveries of the whole case. What did I say? From day one? Prime suspect. Dr Niko Vladovski. Old hook hand. Hang about – you said he was bald 'n all. Sounds like a star swimmin', bear tamin' Russian bodysnatcher to me.'

We stepped inside, through a long shaded hallway. At the end, the apartment's door was already open.

In the flat we found stacks of books, some robes and even a few swords. Everything had a thick covering of dust. Old sunken cobwebs were pinned up in every corner and stretched along every wall, like horrible spider-bunting.

And on the floor, a dried bloodstain – smears and footprints.

'Wise Earth lived here,' Amy said. 'Cold Rain thought about this room. This table. These chairs. This is ... this is where they fought.'

It was clear the apartment hadn't been touched for years and yet—

A sound came from the bedroom.

We all looked at each other, then I slowly pushed the door open with my finger. The hinges creaked.

Everything had been trashed – journals torn to shreds, an old computer smashed on the ground. Someone had wrecked Wise Earth's stuff. Someone—

Detective Pepper pointed at the bed and mouthed, 'He's under there.'

Then he gestured for me to lift it up. I strode forwards and, in one swift motion, picked up the entire bed, mattress, frame, the lot, and held it against the ceiling.

'Guuurgh.'

And there, lying on the floorboards, Dr Vladovski was checking his watch.

'Oh, is that time?' he said in his casual Russian accent. 'I must be going home then.'

I threw the bed behind me, where it smashed into a desk. Then I grabbed him from the floor, picked him up and slammed him against the wall.

'You've been rumbled, ya creep beardy rascal,' Detective Pepper yelled. 'We know everything.'

'You know . . . everything?'

'Yeaaarggh,' I shouted. 'Wheergh maah booddaaah.' No time to type.

'Pardon?'

'Yeah, what he said,' Detective Pepper added. 'Where's Wise Earth? You're in this together aren't you? Admit it.'

Dr Vladovski's feet were dangling, 'Who ... How ... Why are you here?'

'Cold Rain remembers this place,' Amy said. 'Why are *you* here?'

His beard twitched with fear. 'Cold ... He ... he ... Hey, what's that?!'

We all turned and, as we did, Dr Vladovski slipped from my grasp, fell to the floor and scrabbled towards the window.

'Aw, that's a dirty trick, that one.'

Without looking back, he dived through the glass and disappeared outside. There was a thud.

'Ouch,' he shouted.

I went to the broken window, put my hairy hand on the frame and glanced down. Dr Vladovski had landed in a bin in the alleyway.

'Imma say it.' Detective Pepper arrived at my side. 'I told ya so. I *told* ya so. Does *that* look like the behaviour of an innocent man?'

Dr Vladovski clambered out of the bin and towards the car. Somehow he unlocked it.

'Hang about.' Detective Pepper patted his pockets. 'He's got my keys! He's nickin' the motor!'

We all darted for the door and got to the top of the steel steps just in time to see the car rev and screech off around the corner leaving behind only steam, burnt rubber and confusion.

You ever do something without thinking and then instantly regret it? Once, when we were younger, I pushed Amy into a canal after she said that no one likes me because I have a 'simple little face'. She kept saying it, even singing it, and I kept telling her not to. Then, in a frenzy of anger, I just shoved her as hard as I could. Stumble. Splash. Straight into the brown canal.

She lurched up like a terrible swamp monster, screaming and wading towards me. All soggy and shocked. I started apologising straight away because a) Mum had seen and was angry and b) Amy kept promising, with lots of swear words (some of the worst ones), that she was going to do a murder.

The very moment I pushed her, maybe even *as I was doing it*, I was thinking, this really is a bad thing. Yeah. I wish I hadn't done this.

Well, I had a similar feeling that night when Dr Vladovski ran away. It was obvious he was, in some way, guilty. As Detective Pepper said, innocent people don't run. But this was hardly the end of the case – I had, by far, more questions than answers. And if he escaped, the odds of tracking him down were basically zero.

Vladovski still puzzled me. There was something mysterious about that guy. So I knew, no matter what the cost, I had to stop him. I had to learn everything he knew about all this. Ideally, I needed to get back into his brain.

With this in mind, I watched the stolen car drift out into the road, the red brake lights glowing in a cloud of steam, and then I turned and started climbing. Primal instinct, a bit of Tito's jungle fever, took over and I was suddenly on the roof of those abandoned shops. There were about six buildings attached to one another, a long parade – basically a high street.

Thumping along on my feet and fists, I looked to my left, over the edge, and saw the car below. *Three storeys* below. It was slowing at the junction – I could just make out the side of Vladovski's thick beard in the hazy street light. But I couldn't get a clear shot at his mind.

Then he swung the car round, skidding, mounting the curb and revving away along a new road up ahead of me.

Now here's the part I regretted a millisecond after I did it.

I ran to the edge of the building, leapt up on to a low barrier and, grunting and pushing off with my legs, I jumped.

Just jumped right off the roof. I remember thinking, as I flew through the air, past black telephone wires, with the wind in my hair, high over the street below, that I might have made a mistake. As I started to fall and that rollercoaster feeling squeezed in my chest, I decided that I definitely *had* made a mistake. I could sense Tito's body reacting too. It was like, um, what the hell are you doing? Here's a massive injection of nervous gorilla regret.

However, gravity just does not care about your feelings. I came down fast and hard but, luckily, I had timed the jump quite well.

With a brutal THUD, I landed on the bonnet of the moving car. My head and shoulder smashed into the windscreen, my lower body crushed through the metal, dislodging the engine and buckling one of the wheels below, popping both front tyres.

Now consider what poor Dr Vladovski would have seen. Put yourself in his mind for a moment. So he's just stolen a car and assumes he's getting away. He's probably thinking he's on the home straight when, out of nowhere, a one hundred and fifty nine kilogram silverback falls out of the sky like a hairy meteorite. *Phew, that was close, glad I managed to escape from—*

BANG. Gorilla o'clock.

The car swerved, tilted and went straight into the front of a shop. Its wheels rode up and stopped dead against the low wall. But as you can imagine, I did *not* stop. I went flying backwards at considerable speed, carving through shelves and food and drink – everything just exploding out of my way. Imagine throwing a cannon ball at a Lego house. That's the sort of destruction we're talking about.

I landed sideways, right in the middle of the bread section, surrounded by dust and debris.

The whole thing – from jump to now – probably took about five or six seconds.

With a groan, I clambered up on to all fours and picked some bits of brick out of my shoulder hair. The car was wedged in the front of the shop, the engine had gurgled to silence. Steam, smoke and exhaust fumes filled the air.

After checking Tito's arms and legs for injuries (he was pretty much fine – few grazes and bumps, definite sore shoulder, but gorillas are tough), I leapt outside and on to the bonnet again. The soft-top roof came off easily and I flung it behind me. Considering the crash, Dr Vladovski was in pretty good shape too – just a couple of cuts and bruises.

The first thing I noticed when I made eye contact with him was that tingly head-rush feeling. He was trying to mind jump into me.

Resisting it, I roared:

'WHEEERRGGHH ISS MAAAH BO—'

But then I heard a whistle and a thump. Something hit me in the neck. Ouch. *Ouch*. Felt like a bee sting. I tried to swat it. Something metal and hard. I pulled it out and looked. It was a dart. A *tranquilliser dart*. I threw it away. Then I turned to see where it had come from and, dizzy now, dizzier than the wine times, I spotted a large black van parked on the street opposite.

Something was written on the side. Animal … Animal Control?

Aw, not now, I thought, slumping flat on the broken bonnet of the car. The last thing I saw, as I was trying desperately to stay awake, was Vladovski's face. For the second time, I jumped without thinking. This leap of faith, however, was into the doctor's mind …

Chapter 13

The Ocean in the Sky

OK, I'll be straight with you, this bit of the story *is* quite strange. But honestly this is what it was like and I promise, even though it's crazy, it will (kind of) make sense in the end.

It started with a voice.

'... three, two and one ... You can open your eyes now.'

Dark red, almost black. The back of my eyelids. Then two little stripes of white light. Blurry, blurry and finally ... I could see.

I sat up, rubbing my forehead. Where was I? Somewhere familiar. Dr Vladovski was sitting opposite me, in a chair, with a notepad. He twirled his pen. I looked down. I was on a brown sofa. On the wall nearby was a black and white photograph of a bear. Wait. I knew this place. This was his office.

Hang on. I looked down again. I was human. Yes. Yes, this was definitely the body of Chester Parsons. I grabbed my legs and patted my arms. Oh man, such a relief. It was all over. I had found myself. I was back where I started, back at that very first therapy session.

The whole thing had just been a bad dream. I went home and lived happily ever after.

The End

Obviously no, not really.

'That was so weird,' I said, standing up in Dr Vladovski's office and looking in the mirror – I really was back to my old self. 'I had the most vivid dream . . . It was like I left my body . . . and I . . . I ended up in a gorilla . . . I jumped off a roof. You were there. Amy was there. We were filming a TV show. I made friends with a rat. It seemed so real . . .'

I turned towards Dr Vladovski – and screamed at

what I saw. His head had been replaced by a giant hook and, on the end of his left hand, a miniature version of his head was staring at me. It was as though his sleeve was his collar. Looked like a sort of snake-man with a beard. He waved it at me.

'Um,' I said. 'OK.'

'Chester, listen,' the horrible little Dr Vladovski hand-head hissed. 'Do you know what this is?'

'Unpleasant?'

The room was bigger than I remembered. Actually it was huge. Bigger than anything I had ever seen ...

Something touched my leg. A dog. It looked just like—

'Dandelion?' I said – *that's* her name, I remember now. 'Is that you?'

I fell to my knees and reached for her, but as I did she turned and ran towards the door.

'Chester!' Vladovski shouted – or kind of squeaked because his head was so tiny. 'Stop and think. Look at your thoughts. Where are you? You must pay attention.'

'Dude, my dog just escaped,' I said.

Following Dandelion, I arrived at the door, which

was actually a garden gate. I pushed and it creaked open on to a castle roof. It was weird – it was like our back garden but on a massive stone tower.

Dandelion wagged her tail and smiled. 'All right, Chester?' she said. 'Woof woof and all that.' Then, before I could stop her, she bounded and dived off the edge of the roof. 'LOL, laters,' she yelled.

'NO!'

'Chester!'

I turned back into Vladovski's office, which was now Amy's bedroom – I saw a million miles of fairy lights. Amy was there. She was just the same apart from being covered in black fur. I said hello and she grunted. At least I'm still myself, I thought, stepping back to the mirror.

Nope. I was Dr Vladovski. I looked down at my hands. Both of them were little heads.

'Chester,' they said. 'Chester. Chester.'

'CHESTER!' I shouted. 'What?'

I spun round and Dr Vladovski was just Dr Vladovski again. We were back in his office. Everything seemed normal.

'Surely you can figure out what this is?'

'Stressful? Horrible? Very strange? I don't know.'

'You must say it.'

'Say what?'

'Come on, look out of the window!'

'What?'

'Describe the weather.'

'Um, it's raining . . . raining potatoes . . .'

When each potato landed, it bounced, then transformed into a rat and scurried away. A giant wasp buzzed past the window and nodded at me. 'Evenin'', it said.

'*Oohhhh*. Yeah, of course.' I tutted. 'It's a dream. It's obvious now. Dreams are weird, aren't they?'

'But this is a very special dream.'

'Is it?'

'Yes, it is lucid dream,' Vladovski said. 'Do you know what this means?'

'It's a dream that I know is a dream?'

'And you are in control.' Dr Vladovski stood up and walked forwards. 'It is important you listen to me.'

'Why? Actually, it doesn't matter – what's this even

doing in my story? Dream scenes suck. I'm gonna wake up now, bye.'

I started jiggling and shaking, kicking my legs out, thrashing about like a fish on a beach. I did it so much I fell to the carpet. After a few seconds I realised I *couldn't* wake up.

'Chester. It is not normal dream. We are in dreamscape together, you see?'

Perched on my elbows, I looked up at him. 'I don't get it.'

'What can you remember?'

'Um ... leaping off a roof ... Oh, wait, am I dead? Oh, no. I remember landing. Oh yeah, the dart. Some people shot me in the neck with a dart. Tito fell asleep. The animal-control people. I ... I tried to jump into your mind.'

'Yes. And I attempted to jump into your mind also.'

'So we swapped places?'

'Not quite. Best to explain with diagram.'

The wall suddenly changed into a blackboard. Two circles drawn in chalk appeared on either side.

'Imagine if I throw a ball to you, you can catch it, yes?'

202

'Sure,' I said.

One of the white circles flew from left to right, like an animation, across the board. Then it went flying back.

'But imagine we both throw ball at same time. The balls hit each other in the air and fall to the ground between us, you see?'

The chalk circles illustrated this.

'So what, our consciousnesses have collided and fallen down into . . . ?'

'Into dreamscape.'

'Is this bad?' I said.

'No, it is fine. Sometimes it is even fun to do. You can share information, meet in secret, you see.'

'Can we wake up?'

'We can't, not yet.' Vladovski stroked his beard. 'You have been tranquillised. Sadly we are trapped here until Tito regains a little consciousness.'

'Why should I trust you?' I said. 'You're behind all of this. You're involved – you know where my body is.'

'No. I do not.'

'Well, why did you run away then?'

'I did not realise it was you in the gorilla. Your sister said Cold Rain sent you. I thought you were there to kill me.'

'Why would Cold Rain want to kill *you*? Why would ... Actually, fine, I don't care. It doesn't matter. Listen. I'm looking for Wise Earth. He is the key to all this. Please, please tell me you at least know where he is?'

'What do you mean, *where*?'

'It's not a trick question, Vladovski. Where is he? Tell me where he is. Point on a map. Address. Give me his mobile number, whatever. I just need to find him.'

Vladovski turned his head sideways and squinted. It seemed like he didn't trust me – like *I* was the dodgy one in this conversation. 'You really don't know?'

'Why would I lie?' I yelled. 'Tell me!'

'I can show you where he is ... if you really, really want?'

'Yes please,' I whispered, frowning and nodding as though he was stupid.

'Open the door.'

'What? No.' I sighed. 'I'm running out of time.

I'm forgetting stuff. I'm losing myself. Why won't you just TELL ME WHERE HE IS?! Wake up, wake up, WAKE UP!'

The room burst into flames.

'Relax.' Vladovski waved his hand and the fire disappeared. 'The answers to questions that truly matter are always closer than you think.'

'No. No more riddles. I swear if the next thing that comes out of your mouth isn't a postcode I'm going to ...'

'Follow me.'

Dr Vladovski started to float. The ceiling vanished and he flew up into the air.

I was shaking with anger but I had no other choice than to do as he said. I breathed for a few seconds to calm myself, then followed him.

As this was a lucid dream, I knew I could fly too, so I jumped and glided towards the sun. We went up and up into the air, right up to the white clouds above. But they weren't clouds, they were the tops of waves. We turned upside down and were now sitting, bobbing about in a boat on the surface of the water. It was as though the blue sky was actually the sea. As though space itself was a deep ocean and the entire earth was contained in a bubble.

I peered over the edge of the wooden boat. When I stroked my hand through the water, it was warm and glittered and glowed with a thousand dots of white light. A shimmering noise vibrated below us every time I touched it.

'That's quite cool,' I admitted.

'The process of the waking brain and dreaming brain is the same,' Vladovski said. 'Dreaming is what your mind does when it lets go of its senses. When you are relieved of the burden of objective reality. You understand? Here, today, we share control. Here, in lucid dream, we are gods. You want a new house.' He clicked his fingers and an entire house appeared, then fell into the water with an almighty splash and a brilliant rumble of music and light. Our boat rocked from side to side. 'You want to live in tummy of great whale.' He clicked his fingers again and a gigantic sea monster lurched up, or down, turned above us, or below us, opened its mouth and swallowed the boat whole.

I screamed, but when I looked again, we were standing in the entrance to a palace. A huge, shiny, grand reception area made of marble. It was like one of those posh hotels you see in rich deserty countries. You know, where everything is mega new.

'Can we just stay in one place for a bit?' I asked. 'It's getting confusing.'

'Fine. Here is my palace,' Vladovski said. 'I have built it in my mind. I have imagined every detail, furnished all two thousand rooms and weaved in my memories of old country and new. All the wisdom I have. All the knowledge I learn. Here, in shared dreamscape, we can exchange ideas. So I give it to you, Chester. You are free to explore. To know all that I know.'

'An imaginary palace?'

'An *imagined* palace.'

'Gee, thanks. Look, this is all very nice,' I said. 'But did I mention I was in a rush?'

'Time goes as fast or as slow as you wish.'

'OK,' I said, staring at the painting on the ceiling. It was like the top of a cathedral but instead of little naked baby angels and Jesus stuff, there were bears. 'I want it to go faster. I want it to whiz to whenever you just tell me where Wise Earth is.'

Dr Vladovski gestured around the grand palace. 'Young minds, you always look too far for solution.'

I yelled. The palace crumbled to dust and disappeared. Then we were standing in the desert.

'This is getting silly now.' I fell to my knees in the hot orange sand. 'Please. Just. Tell. Me.'

'No, I cannot. You must see for yourself.' He pointed over my shoulder.

There was a tall door with the word 'Memories' written above in neon lights. They buzzed on and off. A door to nowhere. Just a rectangular piece of wood sticking out of the sand dune.

I stepped over and the door opened automatically. Inside I saw a room with screens. TV screens almost. Or like mobile phone and tablet screens. Thousands of them. Millions. Trillions. Stretching up an infinite wall and over an infinite ceiling and across an infinite floor. We were floating like astronauts in the very centre of this place.

'So are these *my* memories?' I asked. 'Just on TV screens and phone screens and stuff? Why are they displayed like this? Seems a bit . . . I dunno, naff?'

'Your mind is presenting it this way – maybe you spend lot of time looking at screen?'

Yeah, true, I thought. Loads of them were broken, like the signal was weak.

'Why are so many of them fuzzy?'

'As you said, you are losing yourself. Soon they will all go blank. Chester, look.'

There was Amy. There was Dandelion. There was Mum. A mad collage of memories and light and colour. Recent ones had a lot of gorilla stuff in them. It was strange, I didn't have to look at them to see them. They were all visible to me at exactly the same time. Obviously this wouldn't work in the real world, but in the dreamscape impossible things happen all the time. Rules like physics and even time itself just don't apply.

'Pay attention to this one,' Vladovski said.

One screen expanded, taking over the entire wall, taking over my entire body, taking over the entire universe. The memory was so vivid it was real. As real as real had ever been.

I was living it. Watching it unfold in real time.

A sunny day. I am an old man. I look at my hands. So old. Frail. I am angry. I am in hospital. I have a cut on my arm. My back is sliced to bits. Oh, I'm a mess. I'm dying. I know that. My long grey hair is red with blood. My black robe is in tatters. I limp down the hospital ward, wincing in pain with every step. I look behind me – there are footprints of blood. This is not good. Blood footprints are a bad sign on any walk. Above me there are long lights and hospital signs. They're buzzing. Fizzing like pylons in summer. I follow them. Then I arrive where I need to be. The maternity ward.

There's a room full of pregnant women to the side of me. I can see them through the glass. Then, on the other side of the hall, there's another room. This one is full of newborn babies. I can see little pudgy legs and arms wiggling in small cots. I step inside – smells like hospital chemicals and fabric softener. So many to choose from.

I feel bad. I don't want to do this again. But I have no other choice.

Through a glass partition I notice a man sitting on one of the chairs. He can't see me but I am free to watch him closely. He has a small child on his lap. She's maybe six or seven. She's fast asleep. She looks a bit like Amy. No. That *is* Amy.

Under my robe I find a leather-bound book. A journal. I step into the hallway and hand it to the man. He takes it and frowns.

There are nurses at the end of the hall now. They are rushing towards me, following the bloody footprints. This is it. Now or never.

Behind the man a door is propped open. Inside this room a woman is asleep. A midwife is wrapping a small baby in a towel. I know now that the baby is called Chester. I take a deep breath in and, for the last time, I jump.

An old man collapses to the ground and dies.

All at once I know the truth. All at once I know that I am Wise Earth.

Chapter 14

The Mighty Jungle

I stomped my foot and everything disappeared. It was just me and Vladovski floating in total whiteness. All dreamy and soft.

'Whoa. Hang on,' I said. 'Wise Earth is ... me?'

'Yes, you see now.'

'Right. OK. Let's just take a moment to think about this. Can we go somewhere nicer? Somewhere more comforting maybe, like home?'

I blinked and we were sitting in the middle of a jungle. There was a family of gorillas milling about nearby and a river moving slowly on the other side of some huge green trees.

'Ah. Interesting,' Vladovski said, touching some

hanging vines. 'You consider *this* home – see, dreamscape can tell you a lot about yourself.'

I could hear that unique jungle music – singing birds and buzzing insects and distant howling wildlife. Leaves rustled above in the warm breeze. The whole place seemed to be moving – like everything in sight was alive. Even the ground.

'This is not a good sign. I am *not* a gorilla. I am ... I am ... I am a nine-hundred-and-ninety-year-old mystic bodysnatcher called Wise Earth ...?' I walked over to some rocks near the river and sat down. Vladovski perched by my side. He stroked the moss.

'Vivid,' he whispered. 'You dream well.'

I noticed he had a Mr Whippy in a cone, flake and everything. 'Can you take this seriously please?' I said, and his ice cream disappeared just before it got to his mouth. This lucid dreaming would have been fun if it wasn't for all the worrying stuff I'd learned.

He pouted. 'Fine. I suggest you look at your thoughts.'

'OK. Thoughts. My thoughts. Right. I ... I have such mixed feelings about this. I'm angry at Wise Earth. But ... but then I *am* him, so ... who can I blame? Wait. I don't remember founding the star swimmers? I don't remember anything before about my third birthday.'

'We tend to hide things we do not wish to remember,' Vladovski explained. 'It is called repression. Can cause big harm. Here you could explore your past, if you wish.'

A wooden chest had appeared on the jungle floor. Above it a neon sign said, 'Repressed Memories'. Near the keyhole a note read, 'DO NOT ENTER (seriously, don't even peep in here – very bad stuff inside)'.

'Looks like I don't want to,' I said. 'What if I just want to be Chester Parsons?'

'You *are* Chester Parsons. Wise Earth has dissolved into you – do you understand?'

'No. *NO.* I do *not* understand.'

'He is *part* of you. Think of him as … as seasoning in a soup. He has woven into your psyche, like you have woven into the gorilla's mind. Elements of his personality shine through – you may have spotted them?'

'Uh, maybe, I dunno. What was he like?'

'Wise Earth had a short temper. He was known to be impulsive. For most of his lives he has done mischievous things – you ever see this in your mind?'

'Actually, yeah, I have. Sometimes I want to do really mean stuff to Amy. I get tempted to steal and, like, I hit some people with a sack of potatoes which I knew was not cool. But I laughed.'

Vladovski turned his hands over and tilted his head. 'You are good to notice – pay attention to your thoughts. Never let them take over, never get lost.' Then he faced me and made eye contact. 'But your character, it forms with time. The genes your parents have given you and your upbringing – everything you've seen, smelled, tasted, heard, every memory, every sensory input – it all goes into the pot. Remember, Wise Earth is just one of many ingredients in recipe of you.'

'The point is to live forever, right? So I can remember *everything* Wise Earth has ever done?'

'If that is your desire.'

'What do you reckon? You're the therapist.'

'Usually advice is not to bottle things up – can make you go full cuckoo crazy. But you are not usual case.'

After a few seconds I decided *not* to look in the chest of repressed memories. I was already quite stressed – didn't want to make it worse.

'I guess all this explains why I'm so good at mind jumping,' I said.

'Good? No, no . . . you are the best.'

On the ground, beneath the long, dried leaves, curled and spiralled and crunchy, a bug hissed and rattled a bit like a cricket. Then it scurried away, through the mulchy undergrowth, up over a log, and burrowed quickly between some huge tree roots, kicking loose dirt out with its hind legs.

A tall bird fluttered down from the canopy and picked up a twig for its nest. Puffing its chest, it chirped a short song, a melody like a harp. Its feathers were every colour I could imagine, every colour there could ever be and more. After a few seconds it hopped away and flew out through some branches, ducking past swinging monkeys as it went. Clouds moved aside and now the sun shone on to the wide leaves above, lighting the clearing green and filling the air with a warm, damp smell.

Although I hated to admit it, this place really *was* comforting. It sure felt like home.

'So what was going on?' I asked. 'The day Chester ... no ... the day *I* was born, Wise Earth was dying. He had cuts all over his body. I saw footprints in blood on the hospital floor.'

'He had fight with Cold Rain,' Vladovski said. 'They used to be best of friends. But they have big ... dispute, yes, big disagreement about how to run the star swimmers.'

All this sounded weirdly familiar. 'Carry on.'

Dr Vladovski plucked a nearby leaf and picked it apart. 'This is a sad story, Chester,' he said. 'Are you sure you want to hear it?'

'I am sure.'

He dropped the pieces of torn leaf and they flew off into the breeze, glowing like embers from a fire. This confetti floated in front of us, animating the story as Dr Vladovski told it. Little red and orange lines in the air, like streaks of light painted with a sparkler.

'Wise Earth founded the star swimmers almost a millennium ago,' he explained. 'He was great guru from the east. He meditated for years, decades at a time. He honed the ability – became Daahsuti master. He taught others the skill. He showed young Cold Rain and Red Fire how to mind jump. But he grew old. So he shed his skin, he took his first baby. Centuries pass, he replaces body when he needs to, the star swimmers maintain continuity, they help him remember. They allow him to pick up where he left off. But soon they transform into dangerous group. He commands an army of Daahsuti masters.'

'Why though?'

'You leap into the mind of priest, of king, of president, of world leader new and old. The star swimmers drive history. Ideas, Chester. *Ideas* are strongest force in whole universe. Every act, great and small, good and evil, starts with humble idea. Like forest start with seed. You'd be astonished how many of history's most pivotal moments can be traced back to star swimmers. Imagine having power to *change minds.*'

'To achieve what? What's the point?'

'Wise Earth wanted to make world a better

place . . . A wiser place. If you walk past a river and see a child drowning, you can jump into water and save them. What would it make you if you stood by and did nothing?'

'A . . . a bad person?'

'Exactly. Wise Earth knew he had power to make bad people good and good people great. He could stop an evil act before it even occurs. His interference with minds started small. A kind deed here, a crisis averted there. And all of it, *all of it*, with the very best intentions. Star swimmers would be like guardian angels. There to swoop in and out of our thoughts and guide us in right direction. But chaos, it throws up unforeseen consequences. To stop war today risks starting war tomorrow.'

'Sounds like a lot of work.'

'Indeed – like spinning plates. Soon, he was just trying to patch up past mistakes. Soon, his guilt was justified. Soon, he really was responsible for more than he could ever handle. And he realised anything less than *total control* would be insufficient. Wise Earth needed more. More star swimmers. More control. More. More. More. But it became too much. Eventually they spent half their time just keeping the order together, keeping it secret. Then this became sixty per cent of their workload. Then seventy. Ninety. Just a few generations in and the star swimmers served only themselves. And did so with ruthless brutality.'

'They killed people?'

'Lots.'

'That doesn't sound like the kind of thing a good guy does.'

'What if you believed by killing one person, you could save a thousand? To practice Daahsuti like star swimmers, you *must* stay under radar. This means no one can know. This means death to anyone who exposes their secret.'

'Why?' I asked. 'Who cares if people know about mind jumping?'

'Exactly – this is *exactly* what Wise Earth started to say. Cold Rain wanted to run the order as they had always done – with iron and blood. He said people, they were not ready. But Wise Earth … He … He said twentieth century and twenty-first century are different. Different in a good way. He said people *are* ready to understand science of the brain. Is it not funny how we can send man to the moon, build vast cities, eradicate disease and yet we do not understand our very own minds? *Consciousness* ... it's the last of mankind's great mysteries, the final question mark. Wise Earth wished to share these answers, this ... whispered truth.'

'But if people knew about the star swimmers, they would get shut down, surely?'

'Yes. Wise Earth wanted a reformation. So he pledged to disband the group, to give up old ways. He, *you*, told all the elders that they are no longer permitted to live eternally. He tried to undo all these years of shame. He put pen to paper to expose himself. The global order begins to crumble. Their power begins to fade. The CIA, the KGB, many people, they start to experiment with secret practice of Daahsuti. He stopped fighting them.'

'And Cold Rain didn't like it?'

'He said Wise Earth had lost his way,' Vladovski whispered. 'He said he grew weak, not wise, with age.

When Red Fire took his side, Cold Rain cut him down like dog and then came to Wise Earth's home. They sat down together for dinner – a civilised negotiation. But it was a trick. And he attacked him.' The glowing leaves formed into men who fought with swords and sparked against each other. 'He almost ended his life. You see this in memory? But Wise Earth knows that he still has work to do. The star swimmers, under the command of Cold Rain, will continue unless he stops them. So, mortally wounded, Wise Earth takes his final body, *your body*. Somewhere he can hide. But his guilt and regret … He does not wish to be the monster he once was. You understand now, why you want what you want?'

A red and gold dragonfly landed on Vladovski's thumb.

'What do you mean?' I asked.

'For as long as you can remember, what have you wanted to be?'

I answered without thinking. 'An actor.'

'An actor,' Vladovski whispered, lifting his hand and setting the dragonfly free. 'You want to be someone else.'

I nodded. Then, as though clearing a screen back to the desktop, I swiped the jungle away.

We were at home now, my actual home, in my bedroom. Dr Vladovski looked around, then sat on the edge of the bed next to me. Everything seemed slightly different – the walls weren't quite the right colour, the smell was somehow wrong and a hazy dream-fog swirled in the air around us. But as I noticed these differences, things gently changed to how they should be.

Dreams. Are. Weird.

'What about my dad?' I asked. 'Wise Earth gave him a book. A journal. Is . . . is that the one we found in the loft?'

'Yes. Wise Earth wanted to leave the old ways behind, which meant no more lies.'

'So . . . Dad knew everything? He knew that his newborn son had . . . had Wise Earth's consciousness in his brain?'

Vladovski nodded.

'But all the pages were ripped out?'

'The journal was his confession. Tales of murder and evil and sorrow. Your father knew that if Cold Rain ever discovered Wise Earth's hiding place, he would come after *you*. And if not, you may grow up and remember and attempt to destroy the star swimmers. He thought the only way to protect his child was . . . was to do it himself.'

'You know, if someone handed me a diary with all that stuff in it I would have just laughed.'

'Your father did not believe it at first. But he read stories of Daahsuti practitioners who were punished. He read stories of the star swimmers who burn my great circus and kill the animals. He read stories of mind jumpers who run and hide. Men like me.' Dr Vladovski stood and strolled to my bedroom window. 'Jack found me when you were still a baby. He tells me these things. He tells me about the star swimmers, the people who took everything from me, and he asks if it is true. I show him that it is. I prove that mind jumping is real. And he tells me he wants to stop them. I warn him. Oh, I warn him they are dangerous.'

The wall between mine and Amy's bedrooms disappeared. I went over to her desk where she had a framed photo of our dad. I picked it up. He looked a bit like me. And then I thought of that endless room of memories. Almost a thousand years' worth of knowledge but only a single image of him, at my birth, seen through someone else's eyes. For the first time in my entire life, I actually missed my dad. A man I never even knew.

'But he didn't listen,' I said. 'He went after them anyway?'

Dr Vladovski stood by my side and nodded. 'Cold Rain ordered the swimmers to take control of his body and poison it. Left poor Jack to die.'

'You've known this all along – why didn't you tell me?'

He took the photo frame and placed it back on Amy's desk. 'I make promise to your father to keep you safe. If you knew whole truth, you would surely go after Cold Rain.'

'Wait, no, hang on,' I said. 'I came to *you* for therapy, remember? You're telling me that was a *coincidence*?'

'Why did you come?'

'Because my mum told me to,' I said. And then I realised. 'You made her say that?'

'I am sorry for deception. Mind jumpers usually discover the skill around your age. You have real potential as an actor. I see you in TV shows, on Puff Puff Wheat Puffs advert. I see your success. I know this path is safe path. I know if you overcome nerves, you will be a movie star. Maybe you don't go after star swimmers. Maybe I keep my promise to Jack. But maybe destiny, maybe fate, maybe some great force draws you to this road. Maybe it would have always been this way.'

'You're meant to keep me safe,' I said. 'So . . . why did you disappear? Looked pretty suspicious.'

He sighed and stroked his beard. 'When the first series of *Amy and Chester* aired on TV, I thought the star swimmers might join dots and come after me again. Look what happened last time.' Vladovski held up his hook hand. 'I had to hide. Then I hear from you and I know we must face them once more.'

'And you went to Wise Earth's flat to wait for me?'

226

'Yes. In case instinct, intuition, pulled you close to that place, in case you begin to remember who you were. I could not tell you, your father forbid me, but I could allow you to see for yourself.'

'New promise,' I said. 'From now on you have to be completely honest with me – deal?'

'Oh, so many promises. But yes, fine. I promise to be honest, unless it breaks first promise to keep you safe.'

'Sounds fair.'

Dr Vladovski clicked his fingers and we were back in his office. I was sitting on the brown sofa, back where this strange dream started.

'I feel your mind, Chester,' he said. 'You haven't got long. You're fading out like candle with no air. You need to return to your own brain soon, or you will stop being you. Already, you seek great forest for comfort. Soon you will dissolve. Soon you will be Tito. Soon path home will be gone.'

Oh yeah, problem number one. Missing body. Still a question mark on that.

'I'll jump into something else, another animal,' I said. 'That'll keep it at bay, right?'

'No. You can't run away from this. Erosion comes with time. With each leap you lose a bit of yourself – at this late stage, stability is what you need. I would advise you to stay in Tito, to only jump if you absolutely must. Parts of you are getting stuck in him – you need to go from his mind to yours directly. This is why star swimmers return to themselves at least once a day. It is gold rule – it is in rule book that *you* wrote.'

I felt like crying. When I woke up, I would be *returning* to a nightmare. It was all the wrong way around. Vladovski had, it's safe to say, blown my mind with all this stuff. But still none of it actually solved the case.

'So . . . so what shall I do?'

'First, you should wake up.'

'How long has it been?'

'A few seconds . . . You will return to Tito, in the back of the animal-control van no doubt. Me, I think a trip to hospital might be in order.'

'Sorry about the car crash.'

Vladovski waved his hand.

'*Then* what should I do?' I asked.

'Do what you said you would. Confront Cold Rain. Tell him you know who you are.'

'OK. Fine. But he said he doesn't know where my body is.'

Dr Vladovski laughed, then tugged on his waistcoat and adjusted his cufflinks (I noticed they were silver bear heads). 'You are nearly as old as millennium,' he said. 'You have wisdom at your fingertips beyond imagination. Yet you still cannot see that Cold Rain, your nemesis, is a liar.'

And then Dr Vladovski was gone. I was all alone in the dreamscape.

I spent a few seconds there, composing myself. Then, with a sigh, I started to climb a ladder made of potential consciousness. If that doesn't make sense (I guess it is hard to imagine in the real world), let's say the ladder was wooden. I started climbing up a wooden ladder.

At the top, I stepped right on to the last rung and, arching my back for balance, I stood straight, wobbling on my tiptoes. The ocean at the edge of the atmosphere was almost in reach – strange sky-water was chiming and rippling above, blue and gold and impossible. The dream-wind whistled below me as I lined myself up, crouched and jumped.

With a slow breath I opened my eyes. Finally, I was awake.

Chapter 15

The Blurgh RAHH Keyboard Smash L3£ afjo3o*vhiirfW:'ap3~]]/->ge4/][+..@{}~

I was on a cold metal floor. I could see Tito's big hand near my face. I wiggled his black fingers. My black fingers. Then I pushed myself up straight and looked around. The ground was vibrating – it tickled the fur on my legs. Vladovski was right. I was trapped in the back of the animal-control van. And we were moving. Driving somewhere.

A surge of emotion – gah, massive gorilla anger. They tranquillised me. I rubbed my neck, frowning and snarling. But, to be fair, they were only doing their job. As far as they could tell I was just a rogue gorilla. Kind of surprising it took them this long to track me down. And, to be double fair, they'd treated Tito better than I had. A few of the bruises from my silly jump were starting to ache, a lot. Poor Tito, I thought, he'd had one crazy night.

Once I was completely awake I tried to come up with an escape plan. I had to get out, then go back to the Whispered Manor. Simple. Dr Vladovski had a point – Cold Rain was *definitely* capable of lying to me. Now I knew all about the star swimmers – about how much control they have – I was sure they were behind everything. And this time I wouldn't take any of his nonsense. This time I would *make* Cold Rain talk. But first, a breakout.

It was gloomy in here. Gloomy and kind of blue from the night. I was basically in a cage which was built into the back of the van. I assumed the bars were stronger than I was and, after yanking on one near the door, I realised that, yes, they were. Made sense.

I turned to the front of the vehicle. There was a small square viewing window between me and the driver – it had a wire mesh. I pressed my face against it but couldn't see anything. However, I could *smell* that there were two of them.

Then, as though I was knocking on a door, I started hitting the metal with my fist.

Bang. Bang. Bang.

'He's awake,' one of the guys said. 'Want me to give him another dose?'

'Nah. We'll do it when we get back.'

I carried on banging.

'Lie down, Tito,' one of them shouted. 'We're nearly there.'

Bang. Bang. Bang.

'*Lie down.*'

Bang. Bang. BANG.

The man's face appeared at the viewing window.

'I said lie down, you damn, dirty—'

I jumped into his mind.

Breathing with my new lungs, I looked around, searching the front of the van. It was good to be in a human body again, but I didn't have time to enjoy myself. I patted my pockets, then checked the van's footwell.

'You all right?' the driver asked.

'Fine,' I said. 'No, actually, I'm not fine. Pull over.'

'What? We can't. We're in a rush.'

'I'm gonna be sick.'

'Be sick in that bag.'

'Look, there's ... there's something wrong with the engine. Can't you hear that?'

'I ... I can't hear anything ...'

'Pull over.'

'*No.*'

'Just ... slow down.'

He eased off the accelerator, but I realised he wasn't going to actually stop. So I opened the glovebox, rifled around inside.

'What you looking for?'

'The tranquilliser gun.'

The driver frowned at me, then glanced at a small metal container between the seats.

'Ah, yeah, of course,' I said.

I unclipped the latch, then took out a small tranquilliser pistol. It was black and surprisingly heavy.

'What are you doing?'

'Sorry,' I said. Then I pointed it at his leg and fired.

'Aargh! GOD! What the hell?!' He swerved, the van skidded and bounced off the bank. Then he slammed on the brakes and it screeched to a hard stop. I heard Tito's big head donk on the inside of the cage behind me – he grunted.

The driver pulled a strange face – it was a mix of shock, confusion and anger. *Loads* of anger. All with a slight wooziness on top – his eyes dipping and rolling. He snatched the dart from his thigh.

'Why did ... why ... That's gonna knock ... that's gonna ... that ...' And then he passed out, his head thudding into the middle of the steering wheel, setting off the van's horn – a loud, constant beeeeeeep.

I took the cage keys from his pocket, then climbed out on to the road. I went around to his side of the vehicle and pulled him off the steering wheel, then dragged him out and laid him gently on a grass verge. We were on a country lane, somewhere in the woods. It was pitch-black, aside from the bright headlights glowing white on the tarmac ahead.

I was tempted to stay in this guy's body, but then

I remembered Vladovski's warning. Parts of me were now in Tito. We belonged together. A direct jump from him into my own body was the only way I could be sure I'd get myself back intact. I needed that silverback. A lot more than he needed me.

After checking no other cars were coming, I went around to the back of the van and opened the main door. The second cage door had a small hatch, about the size of a letter box.

'Who's a good gorilla?' I said, as Tito sat up and took notice. 'You are, yes you are ... Seriously, Tito, I know I've mucked you about, but I need your help for just a bit longer. I promise I'll take you back to the zoo safely when I'm done. I'll buy you loads of bananas and donate money to animal charities and everything – deal?'

Tito just watched me in silence. His big brown eyes were glassy and somehow clever. He looked like he was judging me, his leathery forehead all scrunched up and frowny.

Still in the animal-control worker, I stood on the back of the van, and posted the tranquilliser pistol through the hole. I clambered back down, and unlocked the cage door. Then I took a step away, looked at Tito and jumped straight into his mind.

Now I was looking out of the back of the van at the man standing in the middle of the road – he was painted red in the vehicle's brake lights. He seemed confused.

Before he realised what was happening, I punched open the cage door and took aim with the gun.

'Oh dear,' he said.

Clack, thud.

The dart hit him in the shoulder and he fell to the ground, asleep within a few short seconds.

(Tranquillising people is almost always wrong – it's a bad thing to do. But it *is* funny. I find those two facts quite difficult to fit together. Plus, they started it. Wait. No, those impulsive evil thoughts again. Must remember to notice them. Keep it all in check.)

Where was I? I didn't recognise this place at all. I decided to leave both sleeping animal-control workers at the side of the road on a small verge. There was a blanket in the van which I used to tuck them in nicely. I also left a little note apologising – 'Soz, but lol.' They looked quite peaceful there, fast asleep in their uniforms – one had a wheezy little snore. Sweet dreams, I thought, patting him on the head.

Then I climbed into the van and started the engine.

I had never driven before that night. Not in real life at least. How different from computer games could it really be, I thought. One button, or pedal, is go. Another one is stop. Steering wheel is obvious. Indicating and speed limits and all the other boring rules, none of that stuff matters in an emergency. Plus the van was automatic, which was a good thing because gears are confusing.

I mean, Amy can do it. *Amy*. Can't be that hard.

It's actually quite easy. I managed to turn the van around, crashing a bit, but only little crashes. Fun bumps. That's what bumpers are for – the clue is in the name.

After a short drive I arrived at some traffic lights, which were red. Now I may be a beginner driver, but even I know red means stop. While I was waiting for it to turn green, another car pulled up by my side. The driver glanced along the back of the van where the words 'Animal Control' were printed in big white letters. And then she looked right at me.

As I pulled away, I gave her a good old-fashioned gorilla thumbs up with a toothy smile and the maddest wink imaginable. Don't think she liked it though because she shrank down and, with wide eyes, hid behind her dashboard. But never mind. Onwards.

I made it to a main road and headed back towards Amy and ... and ... and whoever she was with. Were there others? I assumed they would still be at ... well. Um. They would still be where they were when I last saw them. That's where they would be.

Whatever.

It was 2.30 a.m. but I wasn't tired, not after my sleep.

I drove and drove for ages. Again I looked at the clock. It was 3.30 a.m. And yet I still didn't recognise these roads. I didn't even recognise the signs. None of the names of places meant anything to me. Even a huge main sign ... which was pointing towards somewhere called London.

London? Never heard of it.

It was like I was in a foreign country. A rubbish one at that. How far had these animal-control guys taken me? I was ... I was driving somewhere.

Where though? Where was I driving?

Hang on, *why* was I driving? That's weird, isn't it? I shouldn't be driving. Who am I anyway? I looked up at myself in the rear-view mirror. Whoa. Wait. I'm a gorilla. That's not right at all. Do gorillas drive?

Do gorillas ask questions like that in their head?

Very strange.

I had an urge for something. Something important. Something ...

Something caught my attention. A shop. A supermarket. It was closed but a few lights were still on. I pulled up at the front, turned the engine off, clambered out and waddled over towards the window. Licking my lips, I leant forwards until my head stopped. Donk. I grunted.

What was this? Stupid invisible wall of some kind. I hated it.

What do I want? Come on. You know this one.

What do you want? I want ... I want ... some ...
some ...

Food.

Some food! Yes. That's it. Of course. It makes sense
now. That's what this feeling is, I thought. I'm a gorilla.
A hungry gorilla. Phew. Well, this was an easy enough
problem to solve.

I decided to break into the supermarket and eat
everything inside. It was a good plan. Maybe the
best plan ever. What else in this world could possibly
matter? Literally nothing, I thought, as I lifted a nearby
bin and, with a spin, threw it through the window.

Welcome, ladies and gentlemen, boys and girls to ...
Gorilla Time. Fun and chaos in the middle of the
night. Picture the scene – a gloomy supermarket, lit
just by faint fridge lights and green fire-exit signs. It's
quiet. Peaceful. No one is here. Everything is still.

We pan round, we see all the empty tills, the
baskets all neatly piled. Then we see a window. It's been
smashed – oh no, who did that? Outside it's dark, the
wind whistles through the car park. Silence ...

And then the intro music starts. Bad-um, bad-um dum-dum, dum-dum-dum. A spotlight comes on with the beat of a drum. Boom. Then another. Daaah. And another. Dooo. They all meet in the supermarket's fresh-food aisle and sweep up to the broken window.

Weighing in at one hundred and fifty-nine kilograms, he's the hairy, scary, jungle monkey who's not actually a monkey, it's TIIIIIIIITO THE GORILLAAAAA-A-A-A-AAAAAHHHHH.

Rock guitar – BRAAAAAAAALLDRAAA-AUUUUM. And there he is. Bam. A black mass leaps inside the supermarket. The crowd goes wild.

The commentator leans into his microphone.

'Here we go, it's the main event! Now, not many people know this but Tito the Gorilla once had the consciousness of an eleven-year-old boy in his brain,' he says. 'You remember Chester Parsons? Ha ha. No, me neither...'

No, wait, ignore all that. Maybe better like a nature documentary?

Cut the lights and music. Back to silence.

Imagine a quiet supermarket. Night-time. Totally empty apart from a gorilla. Just Tito having a mega feast – apples, custard, sandwiches. He's loving it. He burps and throws a can of fizzy drink over his shoulder.

'Here we see the silverback far from its natural habitat,' the voice-over says. 'He has free rein of the shop. He can go anywhere, do anything. We can see that the gorilla is troubled. Something is on his mind. What is he doing here? Wait. Quiet now. He has spotted something. The magazines and newspapers. He's drawn to the television and film section, curious about showbiz. He surveys the wide shelf of glossy magazines. Primates are intelligent but still, this is unusual behaviour.

'And what's this? He has found something of interest. *TopFilm* magazine. An article about the upcoming *Sword of Steel and Stone* movie. Oh, he doesn't appear to be a fan. Over his shoulder it goes. Another has caught his eye. This next magazine has a feature all about *Amy and Chester*, the celebrity siblings pictured on the front. Why would a gorilla care about such a thing? It looks as though he is attempting to read the words, but they clearly mean nothing to him. Let's try and guess what he might be thinking about, shall we?'

What *was* I thinking? It was impossible to tell. Can you imagine what that might be like? Think about it. How often in your life are you totally focussed on whatever task you're doing? How often are you just watching TV, or reading, or talking, or *being* angry, or *being* happy, or *being* hungry, or *being* whatever? How often are you lost in thought? So lost that you *become* those thoughts. Probably most of the day – maybe even most of your life.

This can be very troubling, especially if you're stressed. Take me for example. Sometimes before an audition I used to get so worried that I actually felt physically wrong. My stomach would be tight, my chest would ache. All this because of stuff that's happening in my brain. And it gets so powerful that I'm not Chester Parsons, I am just a little shuddering lump of nervousness.

Wait, wait a second – the trick is to stop and think. To be *aware* of your thoughts.

But that night at the supermarket, I was truly lost in Tito. Every part of me was pretty much gone. My thoughts were the thoughts of a gorilla. This made keeping track of them very difficult.

At the time I didn't know any of this, but it was happening – exactly what Vladovski and Carlos warned me about. I was forgetting. I was dissolving.

I remember opening a big bag of crisps – I pulled it apart with my strong hands and they exploded all over the place. They were crunchy under my fists and feet. Then I climbed up on top of a shelf and walked along, knocking things off as I went.

'Oh, look at that,' the voice-over continued. 'It seems as though the creature is searching for something in particular.'

I leapt down into a new aisle, weird products all around me.

'He seems curious about this place.'

Looking up, I frowned.

'Wow, he's looking right at the camera. Which is strange because it doesn't exist – all this footage is being gathered from inside the gorilla, from inside his very mind . . .'

Thud, thud, yeah, yeah, la, la, la, la. Being a

gorilla is fun, fun, happy, happy, happy-happy times. Dooby-do. Eating all the foods. Hey. Eating every food. Get the food and mash it in my mouth. Nom-nom-nom-nom-nom-nom—

Wait.

Here, he seems to be getting to grips with his own thoughts. Come on, Tito, you can do it.

Voice in my head? Hello?

Who is that?

Could he possibly crack self-awareness at this late stage in the game?

I carried on walking.

What's this? Boxes of stuff. More food. Flakes of things. Ooh, square ones and round ones. A corn on the cob on the front of the packet. I grabbed the box and threw it away. Not what I want. Another box. Inside I found a bag. I sniffed it.

Carefully this time, I opened it and grabbed a fistful of the food inside. It was crunchy. It wasn't nice, not really, but I felt like I had to eat it. As though something was guiding me here. Maybe it was fate. What does fate even mean?

It was hopeless ... I was gone.

I carried on strutting through the supermarket, eating this stuff.

Something yummy, I thought, turning around and checking over my shoulder – there was a trail of crumbs following me.

Something yummy with smiles?

There, covered in food and frowning, I started to dance. Grunting a slight tune, air coming out of my nose.

'Gurh, ga, gurtle gile gah gah uff eat ... uf?' I hummed. 'A oooohwl. Gah. GAHSHINE.'

Gum gum ... uff uff? What is wrong with me? I need to see a vet. I'm going mad. Wait. Do gorillas go mad?

WAIT.

I stared down at my hand. There, in my palm, loads of little yellowy-brown circles were looking up at me. Each with a tiny smiley face on the front. I ate them. Chewing. Chewing. Thinking. Remembering.

Come on, come on, come on ...

'Gum gum uff uff?' I said with wide eyes.

YUM YUM PUFF PUFF.

'GUM GUM UFF UFF!'

I remembered *everything*. And I slammed the cereal on the floor and bolted for the broken window, now really in a rush. This was bad. Hold on to your memories, I thought, as I skidded outside. Back at the animal-control van, I stopped and tried to concentrate. I even put my hand on my forehead, as though I could keep my thoughts contained that way. Remember, remember . . . the fifth of November?

No. Remember who you are. Chester Parsons. Thoughts. Thoughts. COME ON.

Don't let them wander. Don't get lost. Don't . . . don't . . .

A loud thwuuuck sound – something pinged off the bonnet. I flinched and turned around. The police were here. Oh good. Another noise and the van's passenger window shattered. They were shooting at me. Bullets this time.

'I'M CHESSSTTERRR PAARSUURRNS!' I shouted. 'STOP SHOO—'

THUMP. I spun round, yelling in pain, falling flat

on the ground. My shoulder felt like it was on fire – I grabbed it. Blood – glossy and dark on my black palm. They had shot me. It was a graze, the bullet hadn't gone in, but still, it did *not* feel nice.

Carefully, keeping my head low, I clambered back into the animal-control van and started the engine – I couldn't use my left arm, so flopped it on my lap as best I could. Armed officers were all lined up behind a couple of police cars – luckily, they were so confused to see a gorilla at the wheel they didn't shoot as I drove towards them, faster and faster, honking the horn and roaring. They just stared, chins dangling, heads shaking.

The front of the van smashed two police cars out of the way. One skidded in a circle, the other rolled over completely – a haze of dust and metal and glass, men in helmets running, diving into a nearby bush.

Swerving back out on to the main road, I checked the rear-view mirror and saw the destruction I'd left behind – flashing blue lights and steam chugging up into the air from a broken engine.

Tito kept groaning in pain – I felt I was losing

control, fading again. He panted, making angry, shouty sounds. I needed a distraction. Something to keep him at bay.

As I drove away I paid special attention to my thoughts, noticing that I wasn't sorry, or scared, or even hungry any more. There was only *one* thing in my mind, and it was on a loop. That incessant, infuriating, *beautiful* jingle. Hands gripped on the steering wheel, I sang it at the top of my gorilla lungs – bellowed it out, screaming with the windows down and my chin held high.

Usually it's annoying when you get a song stuck in your head. But that night, those four simple words may well have saved my life. *Yum. Yum. Puff. Puff.* One more time, Tito. One more time.

Chapter 16

Stepping Stones

The animal-control van rolled to a stop at home. It was dawn – the low sky was red, purple, then blue above, the brightest stars fading out, as though they'd given all their light to the sun. Tito seemed to like the sunrise, the comfort of daytime, the warmth on our fur. I could feel he wanted to sit and stare. But the clock was ticking.

Come on, I thought, let's go inside.

Holding my injured arm, I limped up the path. Home was a good place to be, I decided – somewhere familiar, somewhere to keep my memories from drifting away again.

Amy, Detective Pepper, Carlos and Silent

Cameraman were all waiting for me. Up in Amy's bedroom, I answered a ton of questions. Mostly about having the consciousness of a nine-hundred-and-ninety-year-old cult leader in my mind, which involved a lot of shrugging and the words, 'I don't know.' I was still just as surprised as they were.

Dr Vladovski had explained everything to them already (but not on camera – he refused to be part of the show), and this saved me some time. I asked where he was and Amy said he had gone to hospital. Oh yeah, car crash. Of course.

At that thought, I apologised to Detective Pepper.

'You wot, mate?'

He slouched on Amy's bed, propped up with some of her cushions, surrounded by fairy lights wrapped around the metal frame. I was sitting at the opposite end, the mattress springs beneath me completely flattened.

'Sorry, for the car,' I typed into my talky machine, which they'd rescued from the wreckage, then grunted as Amy pressed more bandages on to my shoulder.

'Insured up to me gills, bruv, ya probably did us a

favour.' He yawned, patting his belly like it was a drum. 'Get a saucy new one won't I – maybe some furry dice, ah yeah very nice. Air freshener shaped like a tree, smells like marzipan, ya know the kind. Lovely jubbly.'

'You said it was sentimental?'

'Nah, nah, nah, don't be a sausage.' He waved his hand. 'Only a motor innit. Either way ya jump off the roof looked top drawer. Like an action movie. You got all that didn't ya, chief?'

Silent Cameraman nodded.

'Some naughty footage I bet.'

'There you go,' Amy said, when my dressing was finished.

Closing the first-aid box, she rubbed her nose and let out a long breath – I could tell she had been crying. I guess the news that the star swimmers killed our dad hit her pretty hard. Don't get me wrong, it made me sad too but she was old enough to remember. She saw him get ill and die. Definitely makes it worse to know it was murder. I also noticed the photo of dad had been moved. She'd obviously been looking at it, just like I had done in the dream.

'Hey guys,' Loser Amy whispered into the camera with a sniff. 'As you can see, Chester made it back to us. He's been shot so we're just patching up this wound and then we're going to confront Cold Rain again. This time, we're not taking *any* of his lies.'

Then she turned back to me.

'Let's expose the star swimmers,' Just Amy said. 'I want you to remember *everything*. I want them to pay for all they've done. I want the truth on the front page of every news site.'

I nodded. 'But first,' I typed into my machine, 'let's find my body.'

With a groan, I tried to stand, but collapsed. Tito had lost quite a lot of blood by this point – it was making me dizzy. Worse than wine, worse than tranquillisers, worse than staying up most of the night. But Detective Pepper said I'd be OK. Apparently he had medical experience from his 'military days'.

'You just gotta recharge ya batteries, ya reckless doughnut,' he said, squeezing and shaking my foot.

He was right. I was weak – physically *and* mentally drained. What was the time? The clock blurred, splitting into two swaying pictures when I squinted. It was 5 a.m. Five ... five ... And then it started happening again – Amy's bedroom began to look totally unfamiliar. Even her face – like the face of a stranger.

I shook my head and scrunched my eyes to get a grip on my thoughts – the main themes were fear, sadness and doom. Not good feelings. It felt as though, at this rate, I had maybe an hour left? And the Whispered Manor was well over an hour's drive.

'You all right there, monkey chops?' Detective Pepper asked.

'No,' I typed. 'I'm scared.'

'That's healthy,' he said. 'They say do one thing every day that scares ya. Eat a spider. Run with scissors. Climb a pylon. Fish ya toast out with a knife. Muck about behind a horse. Ya know. Face ya fears.'

'I think you've misunderstood that saying,' Amy said.

'Yeah ... maybe.' He frowned.

'Some things are scary for a reason.'

Groaning, I stared out of the window – even Detective Pepper's rambling nonsense couldn't cheer me up. The sun was just starting to glow over the trees and I realised that today probably would be my last. No more starry nights. No more Chester Parsons.

Carlos scurried across the duvet and up on to my belly, which lifted and fell as I breathed. At first I thought he was trying to comfort me. But he squeaked, then waved towards himself, pointing at his scraggy brown head. I hesitated, remembering what Dr Vladovski said – every mind jump costs a bit of yourself. But, then again, so does time. And Carlos was insisting, now jumping up and down on my stomach, inviting me over. So I huffed, then leapt into his mind. The moment I did, I looked back to see Tito fall into a deep sleep. Once more, I felt so sorry for him.

Chester, listen, Carlos thought. *It's now or never. Go. Face Cold Rain alone.*

It's . . . it's so far away. It'll take too long to get there. (These negative thoughts, like all thoughts, were just arriving automatically – taking over like a bad mood or a catchy song).

Not for the best mind jumper of all time.

We scurried up on to the windowsill and looked out into the world with our tiny front paws resting against the glass. Outside, on a telegraph wire, a small bird sang a morning song.

Jump, Carlos thought. *Jump before you forget how.*

But I lose a bit of myself with each one ...

You'll lose yourself if you just wait here.

I turned back into the room. Amy and the others had no idea I was in the rat's mind.

But they ... they need to film it ... for the show, I thought.

Who cares about the stupid show?

By now I was sure the situation was hopeless – no matter what happened, I would fail. I was going to end up stuck in another body forever. Maybe a gorilla, maybe a rat, maybe that little chirping bird.

But Carlos – he had a point. If I was going to forget who I was anyway, I might as well go down fighting.

So I jumped.

I flew straight to that bird on the black telegraph wire, then straight into the sky. From its mind I dived a mile ahead, down into a cow. I looked to my left across the valley at a sheep. Zip-whoosh. Then back up to another bird, from bird, to cow, to sheep, to dog, back up to a crow, down to a man driving a car, then to another and another, zigzagging along the motorway. I travelled at hundreds of miles per hour across the countryside, like an electrical charge, surging from one conscious creature to the next.

Soaring high through the clouds in the mind of a falcon, above the thick woods and roads and fields and houses, I could see the curve of the earth and the green land below, like a patchwork blanket spread to the horizon. A new bolt of energy now. As long as I kept moving fast, I could cling on.

This was a great way of travelling – I covered the journey in no time at all. The Whispered Manor was somewhere around here, somewhere near the road, across from those cornfields and—

There.

I spotted it – tiny from this height – and tilted my body, tucked in my wings and dived, dived, dived, the wind roaring and screaming over my feathers. Near the ground, I flapped and pulled up, landing on the tarmac right by the gate. I hopped towards the building. Early orange sunlight was beaming behind the black towers and the huge garden was glittery with dew and cold dawn mist. That morning, the Whispered Manor looked like a castle from another time. Maybe another world. Something carved in a dreamscape.

By the front gate, I saw the bald guard, standing there in his white robes – it was the same kid from yesterday. About my age, about my height.

He would do.

That whistling howl and I was in his mind. I looked down at my new human hands, flexing my fingers, making a fist.

The falcon pecked at a twig in the road with its sharp beak, then flapped off into the air.

What's going on, I heard the kid think, *get out*.

No, shut up, I thought. This won't take long.

Who are you? Wow. You're powerful. Are you an elder?

You're damn right, man. I'm Wise Earth. Your ... master. Now relax, I need to use your body for a bit.

I dunno, I heard you were dead.

Right. I grabbed myself by the scruff of my robe and pushed us back into the gate.

'Listen here, kid, this whole place is a massive

stitch-up,' I said with his mouth. 'You've been brainwashed by the star swimmers ... Fred ... Fred. That was your name, wasn't it?'

A whispering brother holds no name ...

I could see this kid's memories – the day they brought him here, all the ways they forced him to remember. Quick, fractured images of Cold Rain shouting, threatening him with a sword. Telling him he could never go home.

'An old star swimmer jumped into your mind when you were a baby. Don't you get it? They literally take your body. Then they take your name away. Your identity. You *don't* have to be that guy.'

There was doubt here. Fear.

'You're scared,' I whispered. 'I get it.'

My parents, he thought, *I ... I phoned them. They didn't know who I was.*

'Yes. It's a really nasty scheme they've got going.'

They said they'd never had a son. No one reported me missing.

'It's all a giant trick – they change minds. They plant false memories. They can control *everything*.'

Ideas ... ideas are the most powerful force in the universe. That's written on the banner in the sleeping room.

'Exactly. Now listen, how would you like to shut this operation down? Expose it.'

I can't ... Cold Rain ... he's ... he's a monster.

'All I'm asking you to do is relax. I will do the rest.'

I ... I ... OK.

And, just like that, there was a surge of peace as we breathed and sighed. We were calm and the body was mine.

Thank you, I thought, as I turned, opened the gate and ran. Straight up to the building, past the stone path, still broken from poor Carlos's fall. I smashed in through the front door, using this kid's shoulder as a battering ram. Then quickly through the stone corridor towards the huge meditating room that reminded me of a church, ignoring questions from fellow star swimmers.

One girl stood in my way. 'Morning sessions are not for the likes of you,' she said as I walked towards her. 'Brother, return to guard duty or you will be reported.'

I barged past.

At the door, I paused. Above, on a red flag hanging over the frame, I saw that symbol – the stickman, gold and stitched into the rippling fabric, looking down at me with all three of his eyes. Foggy memories flickered across my attention, like the fast shadow of a passing bird. Wise Earth designed that logo. It felt familiar in a way that's impossible to describe – a sort of *déjà vu* that doesn't wear off. Only gets stronger.

I grabbed two metal handles and pushed both wooden doors open at once. They swept away, creaking loudly on the hinges.

There were only a few kids in here – maybe twenty star swimmers sitting cross-legged on the red floor rugs. They all seemed astonished to see someone brave enough to interrupt the peace. Mouths were wide open, somewhere between shock and excitement. More of them were gathering in the doorway. Maybe they were keen to see how this unfolded.

Directly ahead of me, at the end of the long aisle, I saw him.

Cold Rain. My nemesis.

I walked fast past the candles, through the still incense smoke, which curled and spiralled at my sides.

He was sitting on his small raised stage, his sword resting on his lap. I went straight up to him, ignoring the confused expressions from the bald teenagers behind me. No time to be sneaky – I just needed my body and I needed it now.

Arriving at the front of the room, I stepped up on to the stage, snatched the sword from him, threw the sheath off – which clattered on the stone – then pointed the end right at his face, just like he'd done to me.

'Hey, wake up,' I said. Then I turned the blade on its side and whacked him on the top of the head.

There was a gasp from behind – mouths covered, faces shocked, more kids filing into the room.

Gradually Cold Rain opened his eyes and frowned. He didn't seem at all scared.

'Hi, Chester Parsons again,' I said. 'Firstly, you killed my dad, which is *not OK*. Secondly, pushing me off that roof? Absolutely unacceptable. Carlos was kind enough to lend me his body and you just ruined it. You crossed a line. Now, I'll only ask once: tell me where my body is or I'll cut off your head. That's not a joke. I will literally chop it off and throw it out of the window.'

More gasps from the growing audience.

'I told you,' Cold Rain whispered, touching what would soon be a sore bruise. 'The answers you seek lie with Wise Earth.'

'OK, let me ask him,' I said, glancing at the ceiling. 'Oh yeah, I *am* Wise Earth. He jumped into my brain when I was a baby. And he didn't tell you freaks which one – so you couldn't kidnap me and shave my head and all that other stuff. By the way.' I turned around. 'The bald thing, the robes. You guys look ridiculous.'

'Welcome home, brother.' Cold Rain smiled.

'Remember the promise?' I looked back at him. 'That I'd return and give you a right good stabbing.' I wiggled the sword near his face. 'Well, here I am.'

Cold Rain laughed. 'And you recall at such a young age – this must be a record. Oh fate, what paths she weaves.' He sounded sarcastic.

Hundreds of kids were standing behind me – word

had spread fast and now the meditating room was packed with star swimmers. Young ten-year-olds, shoulder to shoulder with teenagers and wrinkled men and women. All of them bald. Half of them were whispering to one another: 'Wise Earth has returned?'

'Is it true?'

'Could it be?'

'Who the *hell* is Chester Parsons?'

'A bowl of sunshine, a bowl of—'

'Shhh, listen.'

'You don't believe me?' I asked.

'If it is indeed truth you speak, then you need not ask such questions … You taught me once that the answers we seek are closer than we think.'

'No. More. Riddles,' I said. 'You know where my body is, don't you? You know who took it?'

Smiling again, Cold Rain nodded. 'Oh Chester, Chester, Chester,' he whispered, picking a hair from the sleeve of his black robe. 'Yes. I know who took your body.'

Chapter 17

Locked Inn

'Ah, I knew it!' I said. Which was kind of true – I knew Cold Rain knew *something*. My mind was racing. All this gave me another boost of energy. Now all I had to do was get him to spill the beans. (That's a weird saying isn't it? Spill the beans? If someone spilled beans near me I'd be annoyed, especially if it went on my clothes.)

Although he'd relaxed enough to give me full use of his body, I still felt little blips of fear from Fred. This was, for him, extremely risky. Sure, he could say that I took control and made him say this stuff, but Cold Rain wasn't exactly fair when it came to dishing out punishments. And yet, at the same time, a part of

266

Fred was enjoying the moment – it was certainly more interesting than guard duty.

Maybe it was wrong to wander through his memories, but they kept popping up – probably triggered by coming face to face with Cold Rain. I saw the day Fred arrived at the Whispered Manor. He was nine years old. And he wasn't kidnapped, he wasn't snatched in the night kicking and screaming. No. He simply packed a bag and walked here. It must have been terrifying – watching yourself stand up, go outside, and start hiking somewhere with no clue why. I agreed with Wise Earth. This stuff had to stop.

But even though it was definitely evil, this was a pretty clever recruitment scheme. Keeping the idea of the star swimmers alive over countless generations – getting the children when they were young. Changing their minds to serve the cause. Then sending them out to collect more kids? Man, it was kind of ingenious – even if individuals didn't want it to continue, the system meant it always would, as no single person was actually in control. Wise Earth was right again – ideas really are the most powerful force in the universe.

Dr Vladovski had told me, 'Brain is hardware, thoughts are software – a bad idea is like a virus. It can spread and spread and spread.'

Finally, I understood what he meant.

The grand meditating hall was now full. I reckon every star swimmer was there – a sea of bald heads and white robes, all staring up at the stage, watching this confrontation unfold. I wondered how many wanted to be here – truly, themselves, without any interference – and how many were trapped. Trapped by their own thoughts, trapped by the bad ideas of old dead minds.

But now it was time to focus on the goal at hand. My body.

'Right, tell me,' I said.

Still sitting cross-legged on the ground, in front of the long red and gold flags hanging down the walls, Cold Rain looked up and blinked. And then, with a smirk, he whispered ... 'No.'

So I lifted the sword and held it behind my shoulder, like a baseball bat. 'OK. Fine,' I said. 'Next stop, decapitation station. Goodbye, head. Ready?'

Someone stepped forwards, as though to come to his defence. But he showed them a hand and they retreated back into the crowd.

He didn't seem particularly bothered by my threats. After a few seconds, he even bowed his head, moved his long brown plaited ponytail aside and showed me his bare neck. 'Do what you must.'

'I will.' I squeezed the sword's grip.

'Go on then.'

'I am about to chop your head off.'

'I see that. I am waiting.'

'OK then. Here we go.' I took a deep breath in, lifted the sword a little higher and tensed my jaw. Then I sighed. 'Look. Dude. Obviously I'm not really going to chop your head off.'

'I thought not.' Cold Rain looked up at me again through the thin smoke. 'Weak as ever I see.'

'Just because I won't murder you with a sword, doesn't make me weak.'

He shrugged. 'We appear to have reached a stalemate.'

Suddenly, I felt dizzy again, dropped the sword and

slumped to my knees in front of him. Candles flickered at the edges of my vision, orange flames blurring like a fog.

Uh, Fred thought, *sorry to interrupt, but, uh, is this . . . is this the end of your plan? If so, it's not very good.*

'Please,' I whispered. 'Just tell me the truth. I haven't got long. I'm begging you.'

'The truth?' Cold Rain picked up his sword, then stood, looming over me. If I hadn't been so dazed, I would have been terrified. 'The truth is I *do* believe you,' he said. 'I knew with whom I dealt the moment I tried to seize control of that great jungle beast beneath the garden's moon. There is but one Daahsuti master capable of such resistance . . . and he is you, Wise Earth. My oldest friend. I feared many a winter would pass before you remembered. The truth. Oh, the truth. The truth is I am tired. The truth is leading the star swimmers without your command is . . . impossible. Unbearable. The truth is I can no longer endure the weight of this, this heavy crown. The truth is . . . I . . .'

A single tear rolled down his cheek.

'Um.' This was awkward. I didn't know what to do.

I struggled back up to my feet and, frowning, patted him on the shoulder. 'It's all right, man,' I said. 'Don't cry … it's …' Then I remembered he was my nemesis, so I stopped comforting him.

'*I'm sorry.*' He was blubbing now. Loads. It was extremely uncomfortable. I rubbed my neck and looked round at the star swimmers behind. They were cringing as well – one of them shrugged at me. Seeing this brutal, scary, mean master of theirs break down into tears was obviously a shock for them too.

When I turned back, Cold Rain fell forwards and hugged me.

'No.' I pushed him away. 'I mean, yes. Good. I'm glad you're sorry. For which bit though? You've done loads of wrong things.'

'For everything.' Cold Rain sniffed, then threw his sword down on to the stone floor. 'Wise words. You always spoke the truth. You were right. The things we've done, brother. No more can we darken young minds for the cause of star's light. No more. No more … I yield. You win. I shall remove my elder robes.'

He started to undress. 'Um, no, *no*,' I said quickly. 'Leave them on, it's fine.'

'So be it.' He pulled the cloth back up over his shoulder. 'If diplomacy remains a path we might together tread, I would like to propose a deal.'

'I'm listening.' I felt woozy but curious. Concentrate, Chester, I thought. Hold on just a bit longer.

'As per your instruction, I shall disband the star swimmers,' Cold Rain said. 'Every order shall fall.'

'Good. And no more baby stuff? No more kidnapping? No more mind control? No more murder?'

'If this is your wish, then it shall be so. All I ask, Wise Earth, Chester Parsons, whomever you choose to be, is that you permit me to live the rest of my days in peace.'

'Aw, I dunno,' I said. 'You kind of killed Wise Earth – that niggles me a bit. Also, you sort of pushed me off a roof. And you *definitely* killed my dad. Not sure we can just call it quits?'

'I did not kill Jack Parsons. I never gave such an order.'

'Who did?'

272

'A whispering brother – a silent swimmer. Any one of your loyal recruits.'

'Under *your* command.'

'So high. So mighty.' He wiped his tears away and managed a smile. 'I wonder, are you yet to explore your memories? Over the last nine hundred and ninety years, how many babes in arms have you taken, how many storytellers, singers, scribes and even curious peasants have you had slain for the swimmers and the secrets? If it falls this day, the axe of justice shall cut us both.'

This was annoying. I wanted the moral high ground.

'Yeah but ... that wasn't ... that wasn't me.'

'Who are you, if not the sum of your memories? The totality of all you've seen, of all you've done, of all you know?'

'I mean ... I suppose ...' I sighed. Maybe he did have a point. 'We're going to put it on TV. It's all getting exposed. You'll end up in prison. I can't stop that from happening, even if I wanted to.'

'Do as you must,' he said. 'Fill every screen in the

land with the truth. But fear not. It takes more than flesh and bone, steel and stone, to keep me caged. Just please, do not order my death. Let us proceed with honour and commit the old ways to the past. At least . . . at least permit me to live.'

To be honest, I had no intention of actually killing him – not really. But he didn't need to know that.

'Um . . . All right. Fine. I won't have you killed. But . . . but you're getting off lightly here.'

I felt a strange kind of relief from somewhere, somewhere deep down inside me – a bit of Wise Earth shining through. I guess I had done what he promised he would – returned and stopped the star swimmers. I frowned at the thought – it was quite straightforward in the end. Like driving. Everyone makes such a fuss about stuff, but once you do it, it's like, oh, actually, it's not hard at all. Overthrowing an ancient cult of evil mystic mind jumpers? Walk in the park. Piece of cake. Literally easy.

Maybe *too* easy?

'So wait, hang on,' I said. 'I let you live and then what? What do I get?'

'The answers you seek.'

I squinted at him. 'Just to be crystal clear, we're talking about finding my body, right?'

'Yes.'

'Good.'

'Perhaps a return to form might just put an end to this identity crisis of yours.' Cold Rain smirked.

'Tell me.'

'I shall show you. First, what is your electronic mailing address?'

'My . . . oh, my email? What, why?'

'It is my desire to send you a message.'

'Can't you just . . .' I stopped myself. I'd learned by now that people like Cold Rain don't really do direct communication. 'Fine.' I sighed. Then I gave him my email address.

He removed his phone from the pocket of his black robe. As he spoke and acted and even looked like he was from the past, it was weird seeing him tap away on a mobile.

'Alas, we need not look far for the truths that matter most.' His phone made that little whooshing email-sendy sound. 'There. It is done. I have laid a stone for you on the path you wish to travel.'

'How do I know this isn't . . . I mean, why should I trust you?'

'To Chester, I would say, boy, you have no other choice. And to you, brother, I could never tell a lie.' Cold Rain closed his eyes and nodded, as though in respect. 'Ask yourself who would gain the most from such a crime. Ask yourself what light has come from such dark, what good has flowered from such seeds of evil. Return to your sister, Chester, you will need her today more than most. Now, if you don't mind, I must fly.'

He sat back down on the ground and a tamed pigeon leapt on to his knee. With a slow breath, he disappeared in to it. As Cold Rain bowed his head and slept, the bird flapped past me, darting up and across the high smoky ceiling.

He was right. I had no other option now than to trust him. But in a weird way I knew he was being honest. Those tears were real – I believed every word he'd said. The email he sent *would* have answers. I felt optimistic.

The crowd parted as I walked back down the aisle – girls, boys, men and woman stepping aside and letting me through. Halfway along, they started to kneel. A hundred bald heads at waist height. I was about to tell them to grow up when I realised it was probably a good thing they respected me.

Fred, I thought, listen. I've got to go now. You're in charge. Make sure everyone goes home. Call the police. Get the elders to tell the truth. Whatever it takes. Undo everything. The star swimmers are done.

And if anyone gives me hassle?

Call me. I've left my number in your memory.

Thank you, Chester. I hope you find your body.

Me too, Fred. Me too.

At the wooden cages, I helped myself to a pigeon. It perched on my index finger and I lifted it to my face. Staring into its small black eye, I blinked and heard the wind. And then I looked back at him and nodded.

'Good luck,' he whispered as I leapt off his hand and flew towards the empty fireplace.

Flapping up and up the cold brick chimney through the soot and shadow and then light – I was back outside and rising into the sky. Again I crossed the countryside quickly, surging from mind to mind, from animal to animal. Cow, bird, cow, sheep, dog, cat, duck, motorist, crow, kid bouncing on a trampoline in his garden, squirrel, robin, the pilot of a commercial airliner. I paused here, listening to that cool airplane hiss in the cockpit. Then I stood and looked through the windscreen. Bird, bird, postman, bird, back across the patchy green land below. Zip-whoosh, howl-whistle and gasps from a hundred different points of view. I crossed the miles between the Whispered Manor and home in no time, arriving back in Carlos on the windowsill and then straight back into Tito with a familiar grunt.

Phew.

Groaning in gorilla-pain, I sat up – like waking from a dream.

Detective Pepper was still at the end of the bed and his eyes were closed. As far as he and Amy knew, I had also been asleep. But now, now I was awake – wide awake and about to know the truth. I got to my feet and fists, and knuckle-walked over to Amy's laptop.

With a few taps, I logged into my emails, typing

my password, 'Dandelion123', with my big fingers (I'll have to change that now).

The bold, unread message from Cold Rain was at the top. Blank, apart from a link to a video. I clicked.

It was a short clip from some old sitcom, set in a pub, called *Locked Inn* – a show I'd never even heard of. The video was about two minutes long.

'What is this?' Amy whispered.

I didn't respond. I just pressed play.

We watched it together as Silent Cameraman filmed us from the corner of the room. The footage was just two people speaking at a bar. Two random actors I didn't recognise. It only had eight hundred and thirty views.

By now I was doing a mega gorilla frown, breathing heavily through my nostrils. This was just some rubbish. Some random nonsense. There were no answers here. I slammed my fist on to the desk, growling.

Halfway through the clip a barman arrived and served them some drinks. And then it ended.

'What the hell is this?' Amy said. Exactly. That was *exactly* what I was thinking.

I stayed calm and clicked replay. We watched it again. Searching desperately for clues. Was this some kind of sick joke? Was Cold Rain mocking me? I *should* have chopped his head off. I should have kicked it over a garden fence like a football.

On the third viewing, however, something caught my attention. Something familiar. The man behind the bar in the video – I recognised that face. I clicked it back and pressed play again.

The studio audience laughing, laughing, laughing and, just as the man arrived, I hit pause.

Silence.

And there it was. Low resolution, sitting there in the centre of Amy's laptop screen, all pixelated and small. Cold Rain truly *had* kept his side of the deal.

He was younger, slimmer and had more hair. But it was *definitely* him. I looked to my left, into Amy's wide, shocked eyes.

And then we both turned around at exactly the same time and faced her bed.

'Detective Pepper is an actor?' Amy whispered.

Chapter 18

The Big Shaker

'Oi,' Amy said, slamming one of her many cushions into Detective Pepper's sleeping face.

'Cor wot?' he yelled, sitting up, throwing it away. 'What was that for eh? You're a right rotter, Amy, a right sloppy sausage.' He checked his nose for blood. 'Ah, Chester, you're awake. How's that shoulder?'

Amy and Carlos just stared at him. I breathed slowly, showing my teeth.

'Tell ya what, I could go for some grub,' he said, patting his stomach. 'Who wants to earn five bob? Nip down the garage over on East Street. Think it's twenty-four hours innit? Grab us a pasty and some sherbet.

The dippy one, yeah. With the liquorice. That's ma favourite. What you all staring at eh?'

'You know a show I love,' Amy said. '*Locked Inn*. It's a play on words. Because it's set in a pub, you get it? It was on TV in the 80s – hardly anyone watched it.'

'Ain't familiar with that one I'm afraid. Can I get a' ETA on that pasty?' He looked at me. 'What I do is I bite the top off and pour the sherbet *inside*. Makes a meaty saa-weetie. I call it a Cornish hand grenade – might even patent it ya know. Reckon there's a right big market for that.'

'We saw a video of you acting,' I said, typing on my voice machine. 'Are you really a proceeds alligator?'

He frowned. 'You wot?'

'Guurgh,' I grunted. Stupid predictive text. 'A private investigator.'

He squinted at me from the bed, then glanced at my talking machine, then back up to me.

'Very good question that, very nice.' Detective Pepper spoke quickly. 'I like the way you've framed it. Direct like. Some people would skate about the shop a bit, ya know, tease it outta me. But you, like a laser-guided laser – straight in for the kill. Bosh. Bang. Reminds me of a boxer I used to know. Jonny Flu-jab they called him. Not sure why. Punch like a shotgun. He died in ninety-four. Choked on Lego of all things. Tragic really. He had a bright future. Could have been the champ.'

'You didn't answer the question,' Amy said. 'Are. You. An. Actor?'

He sniffed. 'Well . . . we all act different from time to time innit. Depends on the company, ya know. When ya with ya mates down the bowlin' alley it's all bants, but at dinner with the old dear, please and thank you very much, me darlin', delicious as always.'

'Stop,' I said. 'Just answer the question.'

Detective Pepper stared at the ceiling for a few seconds. 'Fine,' he eventually sighed. 'Yes. I am an actor.'

'Aw, you . . .' Amy huffed, turning away in anger, grabbing her hair.

'Ahll thiiss time,' I whispered.

'You got me,' Detective Pepper said in his normal voice – which was completely different. He sounded like a classically trained actor now, like one of those posh people you meet at theatres. 'Might I ask what gave me away? Was it too much? Was the accent too strong? Method acting is such a slippery slope – the competing for camera time, the exuberant rambling, it all came naturally to the Pepper persona. Frightfully good fun, I must say. It is an old character from my university days. I would love some notes if you have a moment.'

'I mean, yeah,' I typed. 'It was a bit OTT, but I was still convinced. Backstory was believable.'

'All improv.'

'Wow.'

'Why are you giving him compliments?' Amy snapped.

'I'm just saying, he is good. Just because he's a liar doesn't mean he's not talented. What's your real name anyway?' I asked.

'Francis Edward Newton-Parker,' he said, standing and bowing in the middle of Amy's room. 'At your service.'

'Are we quite done?' Amy was frowning. 'Can

we wrap this up? Let's call the actual police and get him arrested.'

'Arrested? Heavens above, why?'

'Um, hell-o, because you're part of a scheme to kidnap Chester's body?'

'I most certainly am *not*,' Detective Pepper, or Francis, said, touching his chest in dramatic shock. 'Red Rose Pictures hired me to act as the detective on the show. That is all. I still have no idea *who* stole your body. I feel somewhat besmirched that you would even suggest such a beastly thing.'

Grunting, I held up a finger to give me time to type this answer. 'Seriously?' I said. 'Think it through. Why would they hire an actor and not a real detective, unless they planned the whole thing?'

I remembered what Cold Rain said to me. Who would gain the most from such a crime? Red Rose Pictures would. A review of the first series of *Amy and Chester* said it was basically the same trick over and over again – me mind jumping into animals and dancing about. They said that once you'd seen one episode, you'd seen them all. I agreed – it was stupid.

The studio said they wanted the second series to be bigger and better. More exciting.

It made so much sense now I thought about it. This series *would* be brilliant. Think of all the cool footage they'd recorded. The drama, the tension, the urgency – finally it wasn't just me taking control of animals for cheap giggles. There was a real reason to watch. There was an actual story now. Me, trapped in this gorilla, desperately searching for my body.

It was all a set-up.

Cold Rain must have seen and recognised Detective Pepper after we broke into the Whispered Manor. He was, after all, a self-confessed TV buff.

'Well, I . . .' Francis stared at the wall for a moment. 'I suppose maybe you have a point there. Gosh. How positively horrid of them.'

'I know you're stupid,' Amy said. 'But are you honestly expecting us to believe you're *this* stupid? How could you not have figured it out?'

Carlos, standing on the windowsill with the morning sun on his fur, squeaked in agreement.

'I was *method acting*, dear,' Francis said, gesturing

286

proudly with his index finger. 'Detective Pepper would have no idea, would he? When you play a part, you really have to commit. Mr Pepper did not know anything about the arrangement with Red Rose Pictures, he does not *know* that he is an actor. Rather, he is an eccentric, hard-hitting detective from East London. To truly act, one must quite literally *become* the character. These nuances make *all* the difference.'

'And there I was thinking reality TV was supposed to be *real*,' Amy said. 'This is a zero out of ten. Absolute stitch-up. But, wow, what a total bombshell. This ... OK. Hey guys.' Loser Amy turned to the camera.

Wait. Silent Cameraman.

I turned too. The camera was on its side, on Amy's desk, and her bedroom door was wide open.

He was gone – he must have legged it when we realised.

'You really do forget he's even there,' Detective Pe— FRANCIS said.

This settled it. Red Rose Pictures *were* to blame. Oh, those sneaky, corporate, money-grabbing (insert swear words here – the worst ones you know). No wonder Brian was so stressed. His bosses were literally evil. They would do *anything* to make good TV. Even kidnapping. Tito's body was giving me another dose of anger. Big anger. I made a fist. I could feel his huge, strong heart pounding in my chest.

Maybe when we arrived at the studio they'd have spotlights and party poppers and an audience and everyone will clap and it'll be like, hurray, you solved the case. Maybe they would have cake? I felt my face smile. No. Back to frown. I don't want cake from them.

'You think Brian knew about this?' Amy whispered, closing the door.

I shook my head. No way – he had been so worried about me. He even offered to stop the show. Brian was a victim too, just like us.

The camera still had the little red recording dot on the front of it. Amy stepped over to her desk, turned it upright and looked into the lens. 'Hey guys,' she said. 'So just to bring you up to speed.'

'Amy,' I typed. 'We're not making the show any more. It's over.'

She lifted the camera on to her shoulder and

pointed it at me. 'No,' she said. 'Now we *have* to make the show. Let's expose the star swimmers, Red Rose Pictures, everyone.' She aimed the camera at Francis. 'What are we going to do with him? I'm still not buying his story.'

There was only one way to be sure. So I jumped straight into Francis's mind and did a quick search. Remembering his memories, I relived his career. He was a failed actor. He did odd adverts when he could, small parts in small films. Worked as an extra. He was poor, earning barely enough money to eat. Also, I noticed, he didn't even have a driving licence – which explained why Amy was always behind the wheel. He was forgettable enough for Red Rose Pictures and, more importantly, he was talented enough to carry the second series of the show. And to my amazement, he was being totally honest. He had committed to the part of Detective Pepper so fully that he actually *didn't* think it through. I had never seen this level of dedication to a character. Amy was right, he *was* stupid – but man was he an incredible actor.

I returned to Tito's mind and turned to Amy. 'He's telling the truth,' I typed. 'And Francis, dude, you are wasted doing weird jobs like this. You're brilliant.'

'Oh Chester, you are too kind. You'll make an old fool blush.'

Even though I felt like I should, I just couldn't be angry at him. The guy's a legend. He was, and still is, one of the best actors I have ever met.

'Well, *Francis*,' Amy said, 'Chester is a pretty reliable lie detector so … would you like to film the remainder of the show for us?'

'What an honour. I would be delighted to. However, I fear they may well be reluctant to broadcast it should you go accusing them of kidnap and conspiracy and other such wicked deeds.'

'We'll put it online.' Amy shrugged. 'The old model is dead anyway, the gatekeepers have fallen. TV is over. We're the children of the revolution.'

'You may twist and shout, let it all hang out,' Francis said.

'What?'

'Never mind.' Amy handed him the camera.

'Spiffing. Jolly good.' He fiddled with it for a few seconds, then pointed it at her.

'Hey guys,' Loser Amy said, with a wave. 'So we've had some bombshells. It's like, hell-o, someone call the cops because we're speeding down weird street. Detective Pepper's an actor – I know, right? Total shocker. Silent Cameraman has bolted. Red Rose Pictures are behind everything. Deception much?'

'NOOOORRRUGH!' I yelled, so loud the window rattled.

Birds erupted from a tree in the garden. Carlos cowered and Francis swung the camera round to me.

'Is everything all right in there?' Mum asked from behind the door.

'Fine,' Amy and I replied at the same time.

'Oh my, I forgot about your mother,' Francis said. 'Should we tell her what's going on?'

'Like, OMG.' Amy ignored the question. 'Chester, chill your socks.' She rolled her eyes. 'See, guys, see what I've got to put up with? My brother is cray-cray.'

'No. No. No.' I typed carefully – it was important. 'If we're doing this then you have to be yourself.'

'Uh, like, lol, what does that even mean?' Loser Amy said.

'You know exactly what I mean. You act totally different on camera. You pretend to be someone else.'

'It is true, dear,' Francis said. 'You do.'

'You ... you notice that?' Just Amy whispered.

'Yes,' I said. 'It's obvious. It's embarrassing. And it's contagious – sometimes I start a sentence with "like". I caught that from you. Like, it's totes annoying and like, I should try and stop but like, I can't? I even call you Loser Amy in my head every time you do it.'

'But ... but ...' Just Amy sat on the edge of the bed, blinking. 'I just ... I just want everyone to like me. Especially now that you're the star of the show. I just ... I just want people to think ... to think I'm cool.'

'Amy,' I said. 'There is literally nothing less cool than *trying* to be cool.'

She sat in silence for a few seconds, as though her whole world was falling apart. As though she had just been diagnosed with some terrible, definitely-gonna-kill-you disease. 'So ... what shall I do?' she asked. 'How ... how should I act?'

'Just. Be. Your. Self.'

She sighed, getting back to her feet. 'I'll ... I'll try.'

We all stood there in Amy's bedroom and nodded at each other. Carlos scurried across her bed, through the fairy lights and up on to my shoulder.

I gently patted my gorilla chest. Not much longer, Tito, I thought, not much longer.

And so off we went, downstairs and into the animal-control van. It was time to face Red Rose Pictures. It was time to end this madness.

'Hang on,' Amy said as we pulled away. 'Where even is Red Rose Pictures' HQ?'

Good point. I hadn't thought to ask where the studio might be based – why would I care? But, thanks to Google and some sat-navery, we were soon on our way. (I know sat-navery isn't a word, but all words are made up. They're just mouth sounds that mean something – say them enough and they'll end up in the dictionary. That's how language works.)

Right. Bam. So we went revving off down our street, took a left and then hit the main road. Amy – JUST

Amy – was driving the animal-control van, I was sitting in the middle, Carlos was on the dashboard and Francis was filming from the passenger seat. Now out of character, he was wearing his leather jacket, jeans, a white vest and, weirdly, one of Amy's pink scarves. The bright Hawaiian shirt was, he said, part of his 'costume'. I noticed that even his body language had changed – the way he moved, the way he sat. What a pro.

After a fast drive, which was windier than I'd have liked on account of the missing window shot out by the police, we were nearly there – according to the sat-nav we were two minutes away.

'I must say, it is a relief to be able to relax,' Francis said. 'Pretending to be someone else is tiring.'

I nudged Amy. She frowned at me.

Turning sideways, Francis zoomed in on us.

'Look at them,' he said, speaking as though he was doing a voice-over for the show. 'There was a certain poetry to all this. The gorilla, the animal within. Then the cautious, social Amy. And we were, of course, hot on the heels of Silent Cameraman, the mute observer.

He was gone now. He had faded away like an illusion, like one's very own sense of self.'

'What about the rat?' Amy asked.

'Hmm, yes, perhaps the rat doesn't fit.'

Carlos looked sad.

'As the saga of *Amy and Chester* approached a conclusion, we reflected on the journey we'd had,' Francis whispered in a grand, dramatic voice. 'In a sense, it wasn't just Chester's search. It was *our* search. Maybe, just maybe, we all found ourselves that day. And now, driving towards—'

'You don't need to do a commentary,' Amy said.

'But I was—'

'Just film – silently. You're actually spoiling it.'

He frowned. I patted him on the leg.

'I *was* about to compliment you on your driving,' Francis said. 'All these miles and you have not crashed even once...'

We came over a hill as he said that and, at the bottom of the long straight road, I saw a building with a large sign across the front of it. Red Rose Pictures, it read, with a bright flower logo. It looked like an office block surrounded by massive warehouses which all had big numbers above their grey shutter doors. Studio 1, Studio 2, Studio 3, and so on.

'And there it was,' Francis added. 'We all saw it together. There was a strange camaraderie that morning – we had bonded, we had—'

'Stop it,' Amy said, accelerating.

Now going downhill, the animal-control van had picked up quite a bit of speed. We were hurtling towards the front gate which was, luckily, open. I watched the speedometer creep higher and higher. But when we were halfway down the road, someone appeared from behind a wall and started to shut it.

'Loooohk,' I said, pointing.

'It's him, it's the Silent Cameraman,' Amy whispered.

He dragged the gate from left to right, blocking our route into the studio grounds.

'Uh ... Amy?' Francis said.

She was *still* accelerating, the engine roaring as she put her foot flat. I looked over – she was hunched at the steering wheel, leaning towards the windscreen like some kind of deranged rally driver who wanted to die ASAP. Snarling and panting.

'Amy, slow down . . . Amy?'

'GUURGH,' I said, grabbing her arm.

Even Carlos was squeaking and pointing.

'I'm gonna ram it!' she yelled.

'It's made of metal.'

But she just kept driving, gripping the steering wheel harder and making this strange noise, which soon became a sort of scream. She looked over to us, then out of the windscreen, then back to us – by this point we were all shouting.

Then, at the very last moment, she changed her mind and slammed on the brakes. The animal-control van tilted forwards, juddering and skidding, skidding, skidding with steam and burnt rubber until, travelling at walking pace, it gently tapped the front gate.

Dink.

And we were still. I held Tito's chest, felt his powerful heart hammering, and sighed.

There was a long, quiet pause. The engine cut out. Nothing moved. Nothing made a noise.

Nothing, except . . .

A creaking sound as the tall gate fell, slamming into the tarmac with a loud cracking thud which sent dust into the air.

'Wow.'

'That right there,' Amy said, '*that* is a weak gate. Zero out of ten. Maybe the worst gate I've ever seen.'

Now we had arrived, I was filled with adrenaline. Raw gorilla-focus. It was like I was possessed (in a strange way I guess I was). Drums, BAM, BAM, BAM, BAM. Everything happening quickly. I jumped out of the animal-control van and spotted Silent Cameraman running straight towards the main building. He glanced over his shoulder, panicked and so obviously guilty, then disappeared inside.

'Hang on, let me just get a good shot of the scene,' Francis said.

But I ignored him and ran, thudding hard on my feet and fists, right up to the building's front door. Bolted from the other side. Not a problem. BAM, a single straight punch sent the door flying, sliding flat across the wide reception.

I chased Silent Cameraman up the stairs to the third floor. He went through another door, stumbling and terrified. Again, he slammed it shut in my face, but I turned it to splinters with my shoulder.

Turning my head, I surveyed the room. It was early, the office was empty – there were just computers and swivel chairs and a few cameras and tripods dotted about the place. TV stuff. Searching, scanning, scanning—

There he was under a desk. More drums – BAM-BAM-BAM-BAM, he took off running again, crossed the full length of the room and disappeared around a corner. Following fast, I found him in the doorway of another huge office, catching his breath.

'It's them!' he yelled (ah, so he *can* speak). 'They broke through the gate.'

I shoved him out of my way and stormed past.

And there, in that office, I saw a boy – fast asleep on the sofa.

It was me.

A man wearing a suit stood by the desk, looking out of the window. This was the person who had taken my body. This was the mind behind it all. Slowly, he turned to face me. Slowly, I showed him my teeth. Slowly, I realised the man was Brian.

'Chest-o,' he said with a perfect white smile. 'You're here. Fabulous.'

Chapter 19

A Gorilla's Heart

My body looked ill – my face was pale and my eyelids were darker than usual. Purple. For a moment I thought they had put make-up on me and I got really angry. What absolute freaks would do a makeover on an unconscious eleven-year-old boy? WHAT KIND OF SICK NONSENSE HAVE THESE GUYS BEEN—

But then I realised I just had tired eyes. Fair enough.

Well, no, not fair enough. Still quite bad.

Brian, all fake-tanned and smart in his suit, stepped over, tucked his arms under my neck and legs, then picked my body up.

He turned around with me floppy and asleep in his

arms. I tried to mind jump back into myself straight away but, because I wasn't still, because my body wasn't relaxed, I couldn't do it.

So, standing there in the doorway, breathing carefully, I concentrated on Tito's vocal chords – I had to speak quietly, but I managed three clear words.

'Put. Me. Down,' I whispered.

Amy, with Carlos in her top pocket, barged into the room. Francis was right behind her, filming the situation. I was glad he was there – catching Brian on camera, red-handed, meant there was no way he could wriggle out of it.

The office was huge, with tall windows and a wide polished wood desk. Everything looked expensive and modern, and there were floor plants in each corner behind his table. I could tell they were fake.

A smell made me frown.

It was a strong chemical smell, a bit like petrol. On the left-hand side of the room I noticed a small store cupboard. Inside was a sofa, food, drink and one of those hospital drip things. That's where he had been keeping me. Seeing the effort he had gone through made it seem somehow worse. Brian must have planned all of this from the start. He must have arranged for someone to take me from the van that day at the zoo. I wanted answers, but first he needed to:

'PUT MEEH DAAAAAAWWWWHHHN!' I yelled.

Brian carefully placed my body on the ground, right in the centre of his office.

'Please stop recording,' he said to Francis, standing up straight again. Then he turned to me. 'Chest-o, darling, listen. We need to take your body somewhere, OK, yah, yah?'

I felt my face twitch with anger.

'I'm thinking maybe near the Whispered Manor?' he added. 'Somewhere far from here. We'll hide it, then we can film you finding yourself, does that sound good? It'll make a great finale. But first, we need to burn everything here.'

It *was* petrol I could smell. I saw a jerry can on its side – the carpet around his desk was stained with the dark liquid. Behind me, in the main office, I counted two, three, four, five other cans – the whole place was covered in the stuff.

Brian was nodding like crazy, his eyes wide and wired up. The guy had gone, it's safe to say, totally nuts.

'You can carry yourself,' he said, looking at me, nodding almost in excitement. 'You're strong.' He sniffed. 'We'll stage it perfectly. No one will know. Oh, it'll look fabulous. The fire here, we'll say that was the star swimmers too. It'll all fit wonderfully.'

'Stop,' Amy said. 'It's over.'

Brian was still acting as though everything was OK – like we were still on the same side. I couldn't tell if he was just bluffing because he'd been caught out, or if he was actually mad enough to believe this was all cool.

'No, no, no. It's just begun. *Amy and Chester*, season three, I can see it now.' He spread his hands out in front of him. Then he seemed to realise that we weren't exactly happy. 'I know . . . I know it's a little unorthodox, darlings,' he said. 'But trust me, yah, trust me. This needs to be good. My career is on the line here, guys. It can still work.' He nodded with too much eye contact. 'Please, please help me. I need this job. I *need* this show to be a hit. Don't you understand? Millions of pounds are at stake.'

Oh Brian, Brian, Brian, I thought. He hadn't been worried about my well-being – all that concern was something else. No, he was worried the show wouldn't be a success.

I remembered what Dr Vladovski said during our last therapy session: 'As you grow older, you will find it astonishing what people are willing to do for money.'

And look at me. Standing here, stuck in a gorilla, performing on camera for cash. I never even wanted to do the show. Why did I finally say yes? The answer was simple. Money.

'You planned it all,' Amy said. 'You got the *Sword of Steel and Stone* people to reject Chester, so we would agree.'

Yeah. Of course, I thought. I *knew* that was a good audition. That role should have been mine. I felt a wave of relief, a warm fuzzy feeling in my—

'Ah, no,' Brian said. 'He actually didn't get the part. I had no hand in that.'

Damn. Never mind.

'And you,' Brian pointed at Francis. 'You had *one job*. You're fired.'

'I suspected that might be the case.'

'I said it was a risk – I knew you'd be a liability. But focus groups tend to respond well to exuberant personalities. Particularly if they're stupid. Red Rose know best.' He rolled his eyes.

'Your bosses are OK with you burning the office down?' Amy asked, eyebrow raised, looking at all the petrol.

'No, of course not. This is my idea,' Brian said. 'I always hated this company – they only care about making money, about big ratings. They've got no appreciation of the craft. We're making art, darlings. The show must go on.'

'Brian...this...this is not all right,' Amy whispered.

'Oh yah, yah, no, no, come on. How naïve can you get? I thought you youngsters were supposed to be savvy. This is showbiz. You're going to get exploited from time to time. You can get all bitter and jaded, or you can roll with it. Need I remind you of your contract, yah? OK, great. Now come on, let's go frame those star swimmers for kidnap – then hit the editing suite.' He clapped his hands, then pointed with his index fingers like they were a pair of guns. 'We have ourselves a TV show.'

'You knew all about the star swimmers too?'

'I've been trying to make a documentary about them for a long, long time. Cold Rain OK, OK . . . Oh yah, he said he knows good television and wouldn't dream of working with the likes of me. He laughed in my face when I proposed an exposé. He said if I wasn't so pathetic he'd have me killed. Spiteful man. But the last laugh is all mine.'

'I bet you couldn't believe your luck,' Amy said, 'when you found Chester.'

'Oh yah, yah, that day on the webcam – a mind jumper the star swimmers don't know about? A gift. A sign that I was *destined* to make this show. Chest-o, you are an angel from above. From the bottom of my heart, thank you. And to take the limelight to the Whispered Manor.' He pressed his hands together as though he was praying and made a quick 'ah' noise.

'An organic, elegant narrative – yah, yah, just fabulous. It has honestly gone better than I had ever dreamed. Now, can we *please* put all this silliness behind us and pick up where we left off?' He held his arm out for a handshake and shrugged. 'Let bygones be bygones. No one died, OK? All's well that ends—'

Something landed on my silver back. A person. 'I've got him!' I heard a voice yell. It was the Now Not So Silent Cameraman. He was trying to wrestle me to the ground. He actually thought he could tackle a gorilla. *A gorilla*. These people were ambitious – I'll give them that.

'Simon, stop it,' Brian said. (Funny, I never would have had him down as a Simon. I kind of thought he was called Alan for some reason. Alan the cameraman. Weird.)

Sadly 'Simon' didn't listen to Brian's sensible advice and, instead, started clawing at my face.

I stumbled to the left, bouncing into a wall, groaning and trying to throw him off. Then I got a firm grip on his leg. Laters, Simon, I thought as, with a grunt, I threw him across the office like an annoying toy.

GAH, STUPID THING. He went spinning and smashed upside down into the desk, knocking it over. All of Brian's stuff – computer, phone, folders and some cheap-looking award statue spread on to the floor.

This pushed the swivel chair back.

It bumped a tall metal lamp.

We all watched in horror as the lamp tilted, tilted, tilted and fell. When it landed, the bulb shattered and a tiny spark flickered – BZZH – as the trip switch cut the power to the building.

But it was too late. For a split second it was gloomy and grey – then the floor glowed blue and orange as flames crawled across the carpet, slow at first but then, with a sudden *whumpf* sound, roared up the walls and over the ceiling.

Panicking, I turned, left, then right, behind me – everywhere was yellow and hot with quick flames and fresh smoke as all the flammable liquid ignited. Within a few moments, we were surrounded by fire.

'We have to get out!' Amy coughed, then screamed as flames lit up on her sleeve. She whacked at them and crouched lower. 'Chester, let's go.'

My body was right in the middle of Brian's wide office, still asleep on the floor.

When I stepped towards it, one of the petrol cans erupted nearby, liquid fire spreading at our feet, cutting us off.

The way we'd entered was now a tunnel of flames, thick black smoke filling the air. Without thinking, I grabbed the desk, which was completely alight, and drove it hard through a plasterboard wall.

Now I could hardly see. I heard coughing – Amy was choking, holding her mouth and shielding her face from the heat.

I picked her up and threw her over my shoulder. Then I turned and grabbed Francis too. I carried them downstairs, out of the front door and dropped them on the tarmac.

They were coughing on their hands and knees, smoke still wispy on their scorched clothes. But they were safe here in the car park.

Again I turned to go back inside.

'Chester, wait,' Amy spluttered. I ignored her.

By now the building was completely engulfed.

Angry fire roaring out of the windows, spiralling into the sky. I ran back through the broken front door, back upstairs and into the main room. Embers were glowing on ceiling beams, which crumpled and fell around me as I made my way towards Brian's office. I could smell burning hair – Tito's hair. Coughing, I held my hand against my mouth and went back through the hole in the wall I'd made. In the thick smoke, I could see three shapes on the ground – Brian, Simon and Chester Parsons, all surrounded by fire.

I knew I couldn't carry them all. But I also knew that, even though they were absolutely not-cool and perhaps my least favourite people of all time, I couldn't let them burn to death. So I picked Simon up and threw him over my shoulder, then grabbed Brian by the scruff of his neck. I looked back at my sleeping body – toxic smoke and heat now screaming up the walls and out of the broken windows.

Again I went stumbling through the main office, falling into the stairwell, coughing and wheezing and struggling to move. I dragged them both outside where I heaved in cold, clean air and dropped them on the ground. Then, with a sigh, I turned around and faced the burning building once more. The red rose on the sign was melting, bleeding down the bricks as the letters fell, one by one, smashing into the tarmac.

My fur was hot to touch, scorched and smoky. My eyes stung and my lungs ached.

'Chester,' Amy whispered from the ground, looking back at the blaze. 'I'm so sorry.'

'The … the fire brigade …' Francis coughed. 'They're … on their way.'

Brian and Simon were unconscious. But they were alive. Amy rolled them on to their sides, into the recovery position.

But what about me? My body was still in there, fast asleep in that inferno.

I felt something strange. Tito relaxed. The flames weren't scaring us any more. There was no panic. No fear. I was calm, peaceful. Maybe even happy. Everything was OK.

And before anyone could say another word, I was running. I looked down at my thick, hairy tree-trunk arms, knuckles hitting the tarmac, left then right, left then right. Inside again, now almost impossible to see. The air was blisteringly hot, like an oven – every time I opened my eyes I grunted and winced. I could hear Tito's throat struggling to breathe, his heart thudding in his chest and the fire louder than I thought possible. It sounded like constant thunder, rumbling everywhere, even inside me.

For the third time, I stepped into Brian's office. I felt around on the ground for my body, then lay flat to look through the thinner smoke. I could only open Tito's eyes for half a second at a time – it was like taking photos. Fire. Fire. Desk. Fire. Smoke.

There. There I was. Asleep on the floor next to a burning piece of melted ceiling.

I picked myself up and turned as a huge beam, hot and orange, fell in front of me. I was trapped. Dizzy, lost – confused. There was nowhere to go. I hugged my body tight, shielding it from the heat, holding my sleeping head and huddling low. This was it. It was over. Every direction was death and danger and pain and—

BANG. A fire extinguisher exploded next to me,

spraying white foam all over my fur and clearing a narrow exit. I squeezed through the doorway, stepping on crunching embers and grunting, patting out flames on my leg whenever they appeared.

Into the stairwell, down, down, dizzy, coughing, carrying my limp body, hoping I was OK, hoping the smoke hadn't done too much damage. Steam lifted away from my black hair as I stumbled outside and, still holding myself in my arms, sat on the ground. I could hardly breathe. I could hardly think.

I just cradled my body and, still wheezing, tried to jump back into my own mind.

At first I thought it was working – I heard a strange sound, like wind. But then it felt like I was falling, like my limbs were weightless. And weak. That strange peaceful sensation arrived. Warm. Comforting. I was letting go. Submitting to it. And it was fine. My vision blurred as I realised what was happening, as I realised what this feeling was. It was Tito.

He was dying.

The anger I had felt about Brian exploiting me seemed ridiculous now. How could I possibly be upset

314

about that when this was exactly what I had done to Tito? Stolen him from his cage, then dragged him through all this fear and danger and pain.

I felt him try to breathe but his body was giving up, shutting down. And then, with a sigh, everything went dark. I tried to cling on, I tried to move, I tried to kick my legs out like this was a nightmare.

With every last piece of strength I could find, I jumped . . .

There was nothing. I was nowhere. But, then:

My eyes burst open and I took a huge lungful of air. I saw the sky filled with smoke. I breathed and breathed, panting and panting. Still lying in Tito's arms, I looked up at his huge black head, which was hanging over me, perfectly still.

Over to my left, I noticed the camera was on the ground, filming us here in this final pose. The animal-control van on one side, the broken gate and the burning building behind us.

'Tito,' I said, shaking him. 'Wake up. *Wake up.*'

His heavy arm was on my lap. I grabbed his hand and squeezed it. He didn't squeeze back. Then I sat up and hugged his gigantic body as best I could. I felt warm tears stream down my cheeks. They were sooty and black. I wiped them away.

'Please,' I whispered. 'Please wake up.'

Holding him, I cried and pressed my ear into the middle of his wide, silent chest.

Chapter 20

The Imaginary Wall

So, yeah, that's pretty much it. A lot of the earlier footage got destroyed in the fire, which was quite annoying. But everything we recorded over that crazy night and morning was still on the camera. Amy posted it on her YouTube channel. As you can imagine, it got plenty of views. Now she has millions of subscribers, so that's good. And Brian was in massive trouble. Kidnap, fire-starting, all sorts of different crimes. Some I had never even heard of, but they sounded mega serious. I actually felt a bit sorry for him in the end, because he wasn't 'bad'. Well, I mean, all right, I guess he was – but he didn't *want* to hurt anyone. He just wanted to make a good show which, I suppose, he did.

Red Rose Pictures went bust after the fire – not because of the lies or anything, they just didn't have insurance on their building. Some probably good people lost their jobs and stuff so maybe it was kind of sad. Brian wasn't very popular with them.

Remember Screentwist? Course you do, the production company that made *Sword of Steel and Stone*? Well, when all this stuff – about Brian, Red Rose Pictures, the star swimmers and everything else that happened – came out, they got in contact with Dave, who got in contact with us. (Dave's my agent who sorts out my auditions, in case you forgot – he's pretty cool. He's also got a pet snake called Jeremy Taylor, which is odd because people rarely give pets surnames. Just thought – I've never taken control of a snake, wonder what that's like? Probably horrible. Just a long wiggly body. No arms or legs or wings. Whoa, imagine how scary snakes would be if they had wings.)

And now they're making a film about it all. I think it's going to be called *The Boy Who Lost Himself* – or something like that. I said they should call it *Chester Parsons is Not a Gorilla*, but they said that was a stupid title. In the movie I am playing myself, which is quite strange, and Francis is playing Detective Pepper again. So he'll be an actor playing a character who is an actor playing a character. Makes me go cross-eyed to think about it. He's also mentoring me at the moment and has given me some great tips.

One of the producers, Harry (hi there), asked me to write some notes on the story from my perspective. But you know that already, because you're reading it.

I was dreading this – remembering everything and trying to write it down – but it's actually been quite fun. Sorry if I got carried away. And I did as you said – I've been totally honest. But only because you promised (promised, *promised*, PROMISED) not to share it or publish it anywhere.

That's still the case, right? You're not getting this printed? It's definitely not getting published at all, even online?

What else? Oh yeah, Amy's got a new identity. Loser Amy is gone, thankfully, but now there's Crazy Amy. Crazy Amy is obsessed with finding Cold Rain.

She's so obsessed in fact that it's crazy – hence the name. Man, she does bang on about it.

I have told her loads of times that he could be anywhere. Obviously, he got arrested, but as you know, he's in a 'coma'. Although really we all know what that means – he's hiding somewhere, in another body, maybe a baby – hey, maybe a snake. He'd make a good snake. I hope if he has got himself a new body, he grows up to be better than he was – and, without the star swimmers to help him remember, it's possible he will.

'Don't you want to find him for what he did to Dad?' Crazy Amy sometimes asks, all wild-eyed and weird.

'Yeah, but . . . where would we even start?'

The star swimmers disbanded and basically disappeared. It was like they never existed at all – proper spooky stuff. There are even people now who think they're made up. In fact, there are comments online from people who believe *everything* that happened to us was staged – as in, totally fake. Like a really big viral promotion for the film.

Maybe that's a good thing? Particularly for me, considering my history.

Fred got in contact. He said that with Cold Rain gone the elders were happy to fix everything – to tell the truth, return all the children to their homes. Basically undo all the bad stuff they'd done. I sort of feel sorry for all those star swimmers – if they really were just trapped there, too scared to leave or challenge Cold Rain, then I guess they were victims too. They're free now.

Although apparently some are still out and about doing their old tricks. So if you ever see a person sleeping on the bus, it *might* just be a mind jumper. Give them a poke from me. (It might actually be a regular person who's tired – if so, apologise for the poke).

I asked Vladovski about that box of repressed memories in my head and he said I shouldn't look at it until I am an adult. Which is fine by me. I'm happy pretending to be a normal kid and not a strange reincarnation of a semi-evil, nine-hundred-and-ninety-year-old mystic called Wise Earth. No matter how you slice that up, it's unusual. (That's another reason I want this to be mostly secret, Harry, because the whole Wise Earth stuff is a bit … I don't know … dodgy?)

After the fire, I was safely back in my body and they kept me in hospital for a bit. While I was there, Francis showed me a photo on his phone. The image of the crashed animal-control van, the flattened gate, with Red Rose Pictures HQ all burned-out and black in the background. Me, lying in Tito's arms. It was on a news website, and the headline of the story was 'Animal Control'.

'See, *animal control* – get it?' Francis winked.

'Yeah, I got that ages ago,' I said. 'Stop pointing stuff like this out.'

There was another thing I was going to mention, something about—

Oh yeah. The other week Dr Vladovski came over and we were in the garden and I saw that he put his arm round Mum's shoulder. I thought nothing of it at the time. Then he came over again – just to see her and, this time in the kitchen, I saw they were holding hands. Honestly, it was one of the worst things I had ever seen. I wanted to attack him with a spade. Get away from my mum, you absolute scum box. But then I thought that was unreasonable. Then I thought some more and even imagined they might get married one day (obviously that's just my imagination and probably wouldn't happen). He would then be my stepdad.

I looked at my thoughts, just like he had taught me to. After disgust had faded away, I felt positive about this idea. I remembered what he said to me in the dreamscape. He promised to be honest and to keep me safe. Those are the two main things really, if you think about it. Maybe throw in 'be nice' and you've got the full package.

Also, Carlos wants to be in the movie – he's actually amazing. Even though he's pretty much all rat now, he still knows some incredible tricks. He sits and rolls over and does all the things a dog does, and more, which is cool. Can he be in it? Obviously, he'd play himself. It'd be better than CGI. Fake rodents always look wrong.

But I want to be serious for a moment and talk about Tito. I felt bad about him. That really upset me. Poor guy. Not sure if he was a hero or a victim or both. But I am sure that he didn't deserve everything I put him through. He certainly didn't deserve to die while saving me. It's hard to explain how attached I was to him – he was so much more than a friend, or a pet, or even family. He was part of me, I was part of him.

Sorry to have such a sad ending – if it's any consolation I feel super guilty about it. From now on I will be nicer to living things. I think we all should.

After giving Mum a big load of cash from Screentwist (thank you again) and my remaining money from Red Rose Pictures, I donated the rest to some charities. One that helps people with malaria in some country I'd never heard of, and another that rescues gorillas when their forests get cut down, again in a country I hadn't heard of – I think somewhere in Africa? Man, my geography is not good. I should look at a map.

As for me, I've been pretty good at mindfulness stuff. I notice my own thoughts all the time and pay plenty of attention to what's going on in my brain and my body. Now I hardly ever get lost in thought. This keeps me pretty calm, so I can go to auditions without The Fear ruining everything. Very handy. Occasionally I muck around with mind jumping, but I am always ultra-careful not to be gone too long. Also, I tie my body to the bed or the radiator or something, for obvious reasons.

I think that really is it . . .

Telling you this story has been difficult, but knowing how to end it? This is nearly impossible.

Shame there's not a cool bit where everyone's smiling and that – you know the classic scene at the close of a movie when everything is all fine?

Let's pretend there was. OK. So it was summer and we were all in the park. Everyone. Even Dandelion somehow (I know that doesn't make sense, but we're just pretending). It's all sunny and warm and great. There's that summer smell in the air – birds tweeting, butterflies, everything. Picture the moment: visualise – we're basically talking about paradise. Then everyone runs together and does a big group hug.

'Hurray. Are we happy?' someone asks. 'Have we all learned a lesson and changed in some way?'

And then everyone shouts 'Yes' together. People are laughing and high-fiving, pointing at each other and doing little knowing winks and fun eye-rolls before they hug again. It's all a bit brighter than normal. Then everyone gets on a boat and the boat sails away towards the sun and then a piano plays and we fade out to black for the credits. And maybe there could be another bit at the end of the credits so some people stay in the cinema even though the lights have come on? Just a short scene, maybe with a squirrel?

Or would that be a bit much? I don't know – you're making the film, you work it out.

I feel like I should say something clever though. Something insightful that'll sum the whole thing up? Something Francis would say.

Um. Maybe . . . 'The end'?

That's rubbish though.

Oh, I don't know. Just remember your favourite part. The roof bit with Cold Rain was crazy, right? I enjoyed meeting Carlos. (Oh yeah, he has an awesome cage in my room – essentially rat heaven.) And the supermarket section was quite fun. Honestly, this chapter is not that good. I'm rambling. It's like I don't want it to be over?

But it is. It is done. Finished.

As I can't think of anything, I am just going to stop typi—

Aha, you thought it was over. Did you know (you probably do), this is called 'breaking the fourth wall'. Talking to the reader directly. Like in a theatre, you have two side walls and the back wall – and then a *fourth* imaginary wall between the actors and the audience. When you knock that down, you have broken the illusion.

This is a bit like consciousness. You are the audience. Reality is the play. And the wall simply isn't there.

(That's quite a cool last line? I mean, obviously I've ruined it now, with this one, but you get what I'm saying.)

Anyway, cheers. Bye.

Kind regards,

Chester Parsons